JESUS SAVES

Up Through the Water
Suicide Blonde
Joyful Noise: The New Testament Revisited

ATLANTIC MONTHLY PRESS

New York

JESUS SAVES

Darcey Steinke

Published simultaneously in Canada
Printed in the United States of America

FIRST EDITION

Library of Congress Cataloging-in-Publication Data
Steinke, Darcey.
    Jesus saves / Darcey Steinke.
        p.   cm.
    ISBN 0-87113-693-7
    I. Title.
  PS3569.T37924J47   1997
   813'.54—dc21   97-16959
                                         CIP

DESIGN BY LAURA HAMMOND HOUGH

The Atlantic Monthly Press
841 Broadway
New York, NY 10003

10 9 8 7 6 5 4 3 2 1

For my brothers
David and Jonathan

But to the woman were given two wings of a great eagle, that she might fly into the wilderness to her place, where she is nourished for a time and times and half a time from the face of the serpent.

REVELATIONS 12:14

One: GINGER

Oh she was high as they flew nowhere in particular in Ted's white Ford with the harelip fender. Her dirty blonde hair whipped around her face. A single strand caught on her tongue as she sucked the sweet pot smoke. Her lungs tightened and she coughed a little, ran one finger down her cheekbone and set the taut hair free, then pressed the joint into the ashtray. Tears swamped her vision and the car swelled gently around her. The light changed from red to a textured leaflike green, as if life itself gestated behind the curve of glass. It was a sign for her to levitate off the seat, slip out the window and fly up, like a piece of paper caught in a whirlwind, high over this place until the houses looked like strings of Christmas lights and the mall a Middle Eastern mecca.

Ted turned his head from the road and grinned. He liked watching pot wing her back into a kid philosopher, when she spent whole days lying on her bed figuring how the earth got here, or wondering if raindrops could be souls falling from the gutters of heaven.

Beside the highway on a treeless hill, between Gold's Gym and the black glass Allstate building, was her father's new church. Ted said the cross on top of the pie-shaped building looked like a satellite fallen from the sky. Her dad's car was parked near the trash Dumpsters, overflowing now with altar flowers, limp gladiola and brown carnations. He was writing tomorrow's sermon, pen poised on the yellow legal pad, willing an angel to guide his hand across the page. He'd scribble for a while, then look up at the bronze bust of Martin Luther. Sip cold coffee. When she was little he'd write about her funny questions. "Was Santa God's brother?" "Was heaven on the moon?" Now he'd decided she'd fallen out of God's favor, he never actually said it, but she could tell in the way he always spoke to her in his church voice, the same officious tone he used with the trustees and the ladies' guild.

Ted turned onto Brandy Lane, dipped beneath the underpass. Cool air rushed in the window and the car tugged out of the dark into a stretch of scrubby pine, a trampled, trash-filled forest, but still charming to her in its familiarity. Her house was in the subdivision just beyond the trees and she'd played in these woods as a child, knew the spot where bloodleaf grew near a dogwood tree and the mossy niche in a covey of rocks where you could keep dry in the rain.

She put her hand over Teds' crotch, felt his rubbery cock tighten. That's what she was after, the dumb thrust of life, like the films on PBS that showed a seed sprouting, peeking through the dirt and lifting itself up. A tiny wet spot bled through the denim—that first pearl of come. She smiled slyly at him and he rolled his eyes in a way that meant *You're too much*. From this side his profile was normal; you couldn't see where the flesh had been torn away or any hint of the thick keloid scar.

Looking back at the tree line, she saw puzzle pieces of rusty brown through the blue-gray branches. Kids, Ginger figured, pretending to be bank robbers or Indians, squatting in the underbrush trying to think like wolves. But the rich patches of color moved quickly and a deer ran out of the woods, all elegant animal grace, weightless and otherworldly. Its antlers grew up into the heavens and knocked down some stars and the deer trampled on them with graceful indignation. The animal's ribs pressed out urgently as it stepped like a zoo animal, depressed and indifferent, onto the road.

"Oh fuck!" she said, and saw from the corner of her eye Ted rear back, his knee straightening as he slammed on the brakes. There was a dull thud, then the sickly sound of blood splattering over the windshield like a burst of puddle water heavy with mud. Her body slammed against the door as the car spun sideways. Black tree branches, the blood on the windshield, and the midnight-blue sky figured and refigured into patterns, as obvious and elusive as a kaleidoscope.

The radio blared. She watched her hand reach out and turn the knob to the left, and the music was gone. Ted cracked the door, rushed onto the pavement, and paced around the front fender, his hands deep in his pockets. He looked small, thin-shouldered, and slight in his unbuttoned black and blue flannel shirt and white T-shirt. She slid over the vinyl seat, came out the open door, and walked to where he stood. The deer was enmeshed with the grill and right fender, grown out of the car like some freakish mammalian extension. Its eyes looked up into the twilight and its mouth was open and filling slowly with pale pink foam.

"What are we going to do?" she asked.

Ted looked up the road to the highway, then down the embankment into the woods. "I'll drag it down there," he motioned to the trees, then bent over and picked up a cracked Slurpee cup from the scorched roadside weeds and pushed it against the deer's glass-splattered belly. "I guess it's dead," he said, jabbing the cup harder into the fur of the deer's long throat. The neck suddenly shifted and the deer pulled its head back, tried to focus its eyes on them.

Ginger screamed and grabbed Ted's jacket, pulling him away from the animal. Its front legs beat the air and the effort sent a stream of blood rushing off the fender; the foam moved out of the deer's mouth with the soft sound of soap bubbles popping.

"Jesus," Ted said, holding Ginger as she leaned against the car and gagged up mouthfuls of warm beer. She puked on the pavement until her stomach was empty and there was just a sour taste of yeast in her mouth.

"It's gotta be fucking dead now," Ted said, adding an edgy nervous laugh, holding his hands over its wide nostrils. "I don't feel any breathing." The deer was still and she watched him stick the cup into the skin of the animal's belly, then throw it behind him, place his hands on the ankles—where the black hoof met with fur—and yank the deer, its skin ripping like cloth, until it flopped sloppily into a puddle of its own blood.

Ted's chest heaved. The muscles in his neck stood out like rope. He jerked the body over the gravel shoulder, then onto the grassy incline where it crushed blades of grass and smeared them with blood.

"Pull the car over," he yelled, "and wait for me."

The urgency in his voice made her run to the car, get in, and slam the door. Ginger turned the ignition key and the engine sputtered to life. She shifted into drive and let the wheels roll forward onto the soft shoulder, then pressed the button on the steering column that squirted blue fluid up over the blood until the window was clear and the wipers forced rose-colored water to collect along the bottom of the glass and flow down the sides. A few small circles of blood remained above the wiper's range, but they were tiny and dark and could easily be mistaken for mud.

She watched the red alternator light flicker, just a short, Ted always said, but it showed how every object was taking on a life of its own, until the steering column had an agenda, as did the backseat and the fast-moving wheels. An empty Bud can jangled at her feet, possessed by wind from the window.

Lately her nervous system seemed like the control center of her body, anxiety shot through her, made her heart pound and the baby hairs stand straight on the nape of her neck. Maybe it was all the talk about the serial killer captured a few weeks back, how he kept chopped-up human bodies carefully wrapped in butcher's paper in his basement freezer. Every day you heard about another grisly murder, and there were always mug shots on the news of the dead-eyed perpetrators and blurry snapshots of their victims smiling on Florida vacations or standing near a Christmas tree. Worry, like cornsmut boils, had grown along the ridges of Ginger's brain until she suspected her body ran on fear alone. She had a bad habit of chewing her cuticles, peeling off strips of opaque flesh around the fingernails, and lately she slept only intermittently, jolted awake by every truck on the highway.

Used to be she could talk herself down by recounting unfathomable odds, imagine one bottle cap on a whole beach full of sand or a tiny star a million light-years away. She didn't know anybody who'd died in a plane crash, or even a car crash. But then she did know a girl who'd been raped—some old guy trapped her in a Hardee's bathroom and did it to her in the stall—and then last summer a dead girl was found floating in the man-made lake. Every night for a week, the local news showed a close-up of a tattoo on her thigh, a red cross encircled with blue ivy. The mushy water-soaked skin broke apart like wet paper. No one ever came to identify her and Ginger overheard someone at church say she was probably a prostitute from California, one of those throw-away types nobody cared whether they lived or died.

Then there was Sandy Patrick. Xeroxed copies of her school picture were up on the bulletin board at the supermarket, taped inside store windows at the mall, even on the occasional light pole along the highway. Ginger had studied the girl's face, her stiff smile and worried eyes. It was the sort of expression Ginger associated with trying to be cheerful when you really want to cry. Just last week somebody found a photograph in a convenience-store parking lot the next state over. An underexposed Polaroid showed Sandy lying on a mattress, her arms tied behind her back, black electrical tape sealing her mouth. Her eyes were closed, so it was hard to tell whether she was dead or just sleeping.

What was taking so long? She saw bits and pieces of ranch houses through the thin strip of woods, sliding doors tinted blue with TV light, bright kitchen windows and murkier bedroom ones. Ted stood in a shadowed patch of trees and she watched his dark silhouette. His hand moved up to his mouth, the tip of the cigarette brightened from orange to red. Probably covering the deer with dead leaves and broken branches, that would be like him, trying to give the thing some dignity. Better than anybody she knew, he understood ritual, how it made you feel better and appeased the gods.

She watched him stand and walk through the trees toward the car. Dried leaves rattled and he broke from the woods and skittered up the slope carrying something white that held light like a sheer scarf. Ginger swung the door open for him and slid over to the passenger side. He leaned in, laid the plastic shopping bag gently beside her, then sat down and started the car, pushed in the lighter, clicked on the radio, fiddled with the dial until he got the metal station, and turned the music up loud. Metallica cranked. His expression was strained and there was something false and dramatic in the way he pulled his Marlboros from his jacket pocket and knocked out a cigarette, matched the tip with the orange coils of the car lighter. Blood was smeared on the bag and she could see the strands of brown fur pushed against plastic. The deer's face came to her slowly, as if rising from polluted water. He pulled the car onto the road and made a wide U-turn back toward the highway.

"You are one sick fuck," she said as she picked up the bloody bag, twisted around, and threw it behind her. The tip of one bony antler rubbed against her wrist. The severed head bounced on the backseat and landed with a fleshy thud on the rubber floor mat. Ted's face was flushed and his thick keloid scar filled with blood.

He patted her knee and tried to say something but his speech was slurred, garbled like it had been right after his accident, before he adjusted to the new angle of his jaw and the knotty scar tissue embedded in the soft inside of his cheek. When he came to in the hospital, his face was a collage of gauze and purple bruises. In baby talk he told how the night had been so cold everything was covered with a fine geometric frost. And right before he passed out, his breath became so solid and white, he thought his soul was escaping. But the particulars, where he'd gotten the gun, why he'd been driving around at five in the morning, and who'd been with him, these things he refused to tell her.

"Well, aren't you going to say anything?" she asked.

"About what?"

"That thing," she motioned to the backseat. Ginger waited to see if he'd answer, but Ted's face was blank and unreadable. The car got quiet; each atom of air grew sullen and mysterious. They passed Orchard Brook Mall. It was an ugly building, the moon a better place for it, not that it was modern but because of its windowless melancholy. And there wasn't a stream in sight, unless they were referring to the drainage ditch along the highway. Ginger had spent her entire adolescence roaming around the fountain and plastic plants, breathing the endlessly recycled air.

Behind the mall the old highway looped downtown toward the boarded-up movie theater, vacant storefronts, and the drugstore that sold porno videos, three for ten dollars. There was still a drive-thru bank and Bamberg's, a big failing department store where heavily made-up ladies sold strange, antiquated merchandise like panty girdles and dusty, cat-eyed sunglasses. Ted turned right, accelerated past the endless parade of strip-mall franchises—the Western Sizzler, Domino's Pizza, and Blockbuster video—then turned down the dirt road toward the dump. The tires bounced over mud holes, past riprap and loamy back fill. Headlights shined over the kudzu-covered maples, made each leaf look shellacked. He stopped near a grove of burnt-out tree stumps and turned off the engine. He got out and opened the back door, lifted the deer's head, and carried the bag with two hands, solemn and ceremonial as an acolyte. She followed him down the hard dirt path, past a pile of tread-bare tires and the carcass of a water-stained mattress. There was smaller stuff too, cracked plastic toys, one like a car's dashboard with a tiny rubber steering wheel. Bits of paper scattered over everything like dreary confetti.

The barn came into sight. "Everything will be cool once I get it all set up," he said, already way in front of her, stomping fast in long, loose strides, leaving her alone in a fairy circle of greasy-looking trees.

Two: GINGER

She pulled one sweaty leg out from under the sleeping bag. Ginger had it since grade school and the material, faded pink gingham on one side and powder blue flannel on the other, smelled faintly of sweat. The ceiling creaked above as her father shifted in his sleep. Saturday nights were always restless for him and lately he was upset about the trustees at church. Last week, she went upstairs to use the bathroom in the middle of the night and found him sitting in the family room reading his Bible by the television's muted light.

She pulled her pillow over her head. Some nights she felt more dead than others. Last winter Ted's tires locked on a patch of ice and they'd skidded into the guardrail. Afterward she'd felt dead, as if she'd passed over to the other side. She felt this way again because of the deer. Like they'd all died. Father. Son. Holy Ghost. They'd been crooked and devious in their paths so their paths led down into death.

The furnace kicked on and the house shook as all the vents jiggled to life. The basement was crowded with damp boxes of family memorabilia stacked on boards in case of flooding. Blue dryer lint clung to every surface and spiders meditated in the corners. Her father's old jazz records leaned against one wall; plastic toys on metal shelves filled up another. Even in the dark she recognized her doll Kimmie, her toy cash register, and the telephone with the eyes that swayed this way and that.

Ever since her mother died nobody slept deeply. Just after the operation, her mother lay in bed, watched TV, read from pamphlets on breast reconstruction, on living with cancer. She cried, sometimes quietly, but usually she'd cry and scream and yell about how she wasted her life, that all the women in the Ladies Guild could go to hell if they didn't like the way she dressed. God was nothing to her and the idea of redemption was bullshit. She never swore, so when she did, it was like a demon inside her. She didn't believe in God anymore. The body, she'd say over and over, was just shit and you can't turn shit into anything else. Liquid built up inside the stitches and when they changed the gauze, it was wet and fetid.

She leaned over, pulled the side table drawer, got her cigarettes, knocked one out, then flicked the lighter, watched the paper ignite and the purple smoke loosen and rise. When her mother first found out she had cancer, she read books about aroma therapy and crystal intervention; she ate brown rice and steamed vegetables and listened to tapes about positive thinking and curing yourself through creative imagination. Her face was always flushed then and her life reduced to anxious waits between doctors' appointments. To her father's horror, she went to the healing ceremony at the local Pentecostal church, had snake oil rubbed on her forehead. When the preacher's hands rested on her head, she said she felt a definite sense of purity and release.

Pentecostals believed that the end time was near and Ginger believed it too. She heard the universe was expanding and this was why time went forward, but she'd heard too that at some point the universe would begin to contract and then time would start backward. The point of change would be some kind of apocalypse, and then all of history would rewind itself like a video. Jesus had the power to make time go backward, like when he raised Lazarus from the dead. This was what was meant by *risen from the dead.* The dead would get their flesh back and be born again out of their coffins and lie in the hospital and then they'd open their eyes and their hearts would start and they'd get better and go home and live all the way down until they were children and then little babies and then they'd go back inside their mothers and melt to nothing and this would go on and on until all of history played itself backward, until people lived in caves again, until they evolved back into apes and then to fish and then tiny amoebae, until everything was in that electrified mud puddle and the lightning would take back its kiss of life and the earth would explode and time would be no more.

Her father was talking in his sleep again, the words muzzy. His mattress heaved sideways like an imbalanced boat and she heard his feet land solidly on the floor and the springs uncoil as he stood. She snubbed the cigarette out against the bed frame, waved her hand to dissipate the smoke, then slid down into the sleeping bag, pressed her head against the pillow and pretended to sleep. She didn't want to talk about God. It was always so humiliating. His footsteps were frantic and reckless in the hall; then the basement door pulled open and his surplice billowed down the stairs. *Had he slept in his church robes?* But once her eyes adjusted, she saw it was just a pile of dirty sheets draped down the steps and a cold draft caught in the stairwell, shifting and rattling the door on its hinges. He was still in bed, restlessly rolling sideways, yelling out, "Her spilled blood will pass for moonlight."

Amen, Ginger thought, *crucify the flesh.* She reached out from under the flannel and grabbed the lighter, pushed her thumb against the flint; a tiny sunset appeared, blue-green core, the arch of transparent orange and creamy wavering light on top. She brought that flame so close to her eye she felt its moisture heat up and evaporate. *Jesus come down,* she prayed, *and save us from our miserable selves.*

Ginger's T-shirt twisted around her sweaty stomach and blood swelled against her temple. She opened her eyes. In the dream she'd approached the deer in the woods, slowly, with her hand outstretched, like when she was little and wanted to get close to rabbits or birds. The deer reached out its front leg; the black hoof curving around her fingers like soft tar.

Her father was talking upstairs, practicing his sermon, trying to convert the medicine cabinet. It wasn't eight yet, but he'd been up for hours and she'd heard his footfalls creeping around the kitchen as he had his long meditative breakfast of black coffee and buttered toast. Sometimes he'd sneak cigarettes and play his jazz records, the volume just barely audible.

Last night's red wine pickled her mouth and she felt fragile. Her breasts were sore and there was that mysterious feeling in her lower stomach. But the blood and the horrible cramps were still a week away. Sometimes they got so bad she felt like she was fighting an invisible adversary, one that punched her in the stomach and then reached up into her gut.

It was Sunday morning. The air told her, as did the light. Every object looked hollow and inconsequential. Today the material world was little comfort and she felt anxiety rise in her chest until she had to muffle a cough. She couldn't decipher his words, but she listened to his voice rise and fall theatrically, tried to judge if he had butterflies in his stomach. "It never gets any easier," he'd say to her if she caught him coming out of the bathroom, the blood drained from his face, nervousness widening his pupils.

She listened to him walk down the carpeted hallway, back into the kitchen, where he paused to put on his long black coat, pick up his Oxford English Bible with the sermon pressed inside, and leave the house through the kitchen door. He started the car, but it wasn't until Ginger heard him back up and accelerate down the road that she threw off the sleeping bag, pulled up her jeans, and climbed the dark stairwell into the light of the house.

His breakfast dishes sat in the sink and she washed them, gazing out the window through the gray woods to the cars, blurs of metallic color rushed by on the highway. She got a cup of burnt coffee and sat in the family room, used the remote to turn on the TV. There was a fat little man with a lacquered hairpiece saying *Be healed* on one station and the technicolor Bible story of the ten commandments on another. She looked at the religious paintings behind her. One showed a dank and rotting woods but as you followed the trunks up, the sick leaves turned to Easter lilies and the light was pale and blue at the top. The other was of a little ark, floating on a dark and dangerous river. On a marble shelf below was the soapstone bust of an African woman a missionary had given to her mother.

She rose in a languid way, like a person morally oppressed by heat, and staggered down the hall to her father's room, lay over his unmade bed, then opened his closet. Most of his clothes were black, short- and long-sleeved minister shirts and plain black pants. In the drawers were T-shirts, some with worn logos from former church softball teams, his white underwear, and endless pairs of mismatched black socks. In the top drawer was a leather box, and she took it to the bed and opened it. Inside were horsehide cuff links from when he was a boy and the Celtic cross her mother gave him for a wedding present, a tiny cross lapel pin he wore in the hospital, and a yellowed newspaper clipping from his ordination, pennies, paper clips, and one German coin.

She closed the box, careful to return everything to its original place, then walked across the hall to her old room and flung herself onto the bed. The room was painted pale peach and there was a pressed-wood chest and desk, both painted white, and a pink rug in a hue her mother called salmon. While she was sick her mother slept here and the smell of ammonia clung to the curtains. At the very end her mother became sweet like a baby, blank-eyed, talking gibberish. After morphine, her lids drooped and she'd sleep. But an hour later she'd arch her back and scream until the nurse had to strap her in a white muslin jacket with metal hooks that held her to the bed frame.

At first her father sat at her mother's side, held her hand, sometimes touching her flushed cheek, the edges of his mouth turned down with sympathy and his eyes glassy and red. He'd nod his head, agreeing with everything she said, about how unfair life was, how it didn't seem to make any sense. Sometimes he'd say something about the mysteries of God's Will, about cultivating strong faith, and her mother would get angry and ask him to leave the room, say she didn't like to hear him talk nonsense. Near the end, her eyes grew wild and desperate; she'd called him in to pray, but she wouldn't hold his hand, kept insisting that he grasp the hand of Ginger's old teddy bear. He'd finally relented and bowed his head, his body brittle with embarrassment. Her mother didn't believe in God anymore and she just laughed. After that, he rarely came into the room, just hovered at the doorway, asking the nurse if she needed anything.

Ginger opened the closet and took down the shoe box from the top shelf that held all of the sympathy cards they received when her mother died. Most had little animals on them, blue birds and bunnies, or a Jesus in soft focus looking wise and demure. One woman wrote in a shaky cursive script that God needed her mother in heaven, that he'd looked down from the clouds, seen her suffering, and decided she'd be better off with him. She took a skirt from a hanger and pulled it up around her waist, fastened the button. The floral skirt was the one piece of her mother's clothing she'd kept and though she knew the people at the church thought she was crazy, she wore it there almost every week.

She needed to hurry; if she wanted to get to church before the sermon, she'd have to start walking now. It was late enough to walk along the highway in peace, without members stopping to ask if she needed a ride.

* * *

The hymn swelled, one of the old ones, its melody ponder-
ous and Germanic. The usher pressed a bulletin into her hand and she
slid into the last pew, a position saved for latecomers like herself. She
was lucky. There weren't many typos in the bulletin this week. In the
announcements that counted—the special thank you to Herb Clayton
for making and donating the guest-book stand in the narthex, and the
notice for the youth group dinner featuring corn dogs, and the Martin
Luther movie Wednesday night—everything was spelled correctly.
She'd seen that movie a hundred times, always admiring Martin's short
earnest hair-do and the part when rain blew in the window and he
fainted because he was so afraid of God. The altar flowers, white
carnations, yellow mums, red gladiola in a pulp paper vase, were given
by Mr. Mulhoffer in memory of his beloved mother, the legendary
Eva Mulhoffer, whose sauerbraten was as important to the history of
the church as the founding ministers. It was Mulhoffer who put up the
money for this new church. He argued in congregational meetings that
the downtown area was dead, filled with drug addicts and petty crimi-
nals and that the future of the church was in the suburbs, where his
pressed-wood furniture factory was located, down the highway, not
far from the interstate entrance. He'd made a fortune in cheap colonial bedroom sets, Formica dinettes, couches that looked like overweight lazy-boy recliners. It was junky stuff, but Mr. Mulhoffer was
not an unappealing man. He wore his white hair short and his pants
pulled up over his big belly, and he was charming and friendly to everyone. But Ginger didn't like him because he believed unequivocally
that anything new was better than anything old. His wife shared her
husband's fanatical love of the new. Every Saturday she came by the
church to urge Ginger's father to wear the new vestments, the mini-

mal alb and the thin red stole with the machine-embroidered Alpha and Omega. Her father told Ginger that in the new vestments he felt like an alien in a bad sci-fi movie.

She watched him sitting on the wood slab suspended from the white brick wall, jotting down notes on the pages of his sermon. He looked anachronistic in his silk-lined robe, the cuffs edged with ornate lace; these vestments looked better in the old stone church, with the detailed cherry-wood altar and the gold glass lanterns hanging from the ceiling.

The organist pressed hard on the crescendo shoe and the congregation bellowed.

> *And though they take our life / goods, honor, children, wife / yet is their profit small / these things shall vanish all / the city of God remaineth.*

The lights dimmed for the sermon. The stained-glass windows cast red, yellow, and lime green auras over members sitting at the edge of the pews. She'd never get used to the white brick walls and geometric stained-glass windows of the new church. Her father told her the building was modeled after some modern church in France. The original probably had an exotic feel, Mediterranean or Middle Eastern, but this replica, with its track lighting and wall-to-wall red carpeting, felt generic as an airport.

Her father made his way up into the pulpit, laid down his Oxford English Bible, spread out his sermon, flattened the folded crease with his hand, and put on his half-lens reading glasses. He was handsome in a faded Scandinavian sort of way, with his long face and

Darcey Steinke

high coloring. She sat up so the points of her spine rested against the wood pew, aware that she hadn't showered and still smelled of smoke and sex.

Bowing his head, her father intoned, "Lord, we offer this message in the name of your son Jesus Christ our Savior, Amen." He looked over the members, his face relaxed, somewhat confessional. "You know, you can learn a lot from studying dreams. Last night I had a dream. I was driving cross-country, my eyes strained by the piercing headlights of cars in the opposite lane and the monotony of the highway. From a thermos I poured and drank one cup of black coffee after another. I had no real idea of my cargo or my destination. Whenever I glanced up through the top of the windshield into the starry night, I saw the silhouettes of ravens curving wide figure eights.

"In the deepest part of the night, I needed a break, veered off the highway into a rest stop, got out, and walked around the back of the van. As I looked up at the deserted brick pavilion that housed a bevy of snack machines, it occurred to me that I had to be careful, that I didn't want anyone to see my cargo, and that's when I realized Sandy Patrick was inside the van and that it was I who had kidnapped her." The pews creaked as the congregation shifted uncomfortably.

"But how could this be? I had no memory of the kidnapping, no memory even of loading the girl into the van. My first impulse was to move away from the van, then run out into the highway, stick out my thumb, and try to hitchhike home. But then a sound came from inside the van; curiosity overwhelmed my fear and I unlocked the back doors and pulled both open. Laying on the cold metal floor was a body. Flesh so pale it glowed a fuzzy blue and seemed to hover

20

in the dark. The white bloodless feet and purple toenails were clos-est to me, ankles bound with polyester cord. I was relieved, for it was not a woman's body but a man's. Head shaved, one eye badly bruised and swollen shut. Dried blood obscured his features; clear packing tape flattened his mouth and distorted his lips. But the ruined face was familiar and as I studied the features, I realized it was Jesus Christ our Lord and Savior. Looking at him I had a feeling of such fear and complicity that I woke up screaming.

"For hours I lay awake, trying to decipher the dream. Am I complicit? Small things happen. We tell fibs, withhold love, cheat on taxes, use condescension and hasty class consciousness to shame both strangers and friends. Do these minor sins multiply and allow evil into our world? Could I be complicit in something as macabre as the abduction of Sandy Patrick?

"Who here does not know the story of Sandy Patrick?" He looked at the faces in pew after pew as if somebody might actually answer. "Her mother says she has a dreamy side, that she collects stuffed animals, reads fantasy novels where horses fly and fairy prin-cesses wear gowns made from flowers. Neighbors told reporters that she's a shy but loving child, always bringing home stray cats. One lady remembers how she took in a hurt bird, kept it in a shoe box, and force-fed it dog food on a Popsicle stick.

"But can this sensitive girl be a suitable stand-in for Christ? Must I accept my complicity in her abduction? Does each one of us have to come to terms with the evil that resides within us?

"The answer to both questions is of course yes. Yes, this girl, all rainbows and unicorns, is Christ. Just as much as that tiny baby in the manger was our savior. And yes, each of us must look into our hearts and acknowledge the darkness there. That's the shocking truth!

The evil power that abducted Sandy is not just the exception to the rule but rather part of the fabric of human reality, of our reality, a dark fabric with which we are all clothed and which we cannot cast off. Each of us is scarred with the inheritance of Adam and Eve, that tainted couple who separated themselves from God, who began our long and bloody journey.

"So let us remember Sandy Patrick in an aura of divine light. Let us pray for her in hope that her pain will not be wasted, that in turn it will work as an elixir, just as Christ's blood does in communion, to turn our black hearts pure and white as the first winter snow. In the name of our Lord Jesus Christ, Amen."

The organist played the first chords of the next hymn. Ginger watched as Mrs. Mulhoffer moved discreetly out of the front pew and down the side aisle. Several other people edged out of their seats, following her, all their expressions tense with outrage and indignation. She heard a woman whisper to her husband, "How dare he say we killed that little girl." Ginger'd heard them talk; they said that Ruth Patrick deserved what she got, that she was one of the divorcees that got drunk on singles' night at the Holiday Inn Lounge and that she took continuing education classes just to meet men. The ushers passed the red velvet offering bag from pew to pew.

Sandy'd been gone for months. Dread shivered up Ginger's spine. It seemed like bad luck to mention her. The ushers, jovial and unfazed, walked in formation down the center aisle, carrying red bags of green money and checks. All four could be brothers in their dark suits with the brocade Maltese Cross pocket patch. They shared the same temperament too, self-deprecating and funny; Ginger liked how they joked with her about oversleeping and how during the sermon they slipped outside to smoke.

Her father took the bags, settling each on top of the other. Then held all four up and with a little prayer, he consecrated the cash for Jesus. She pitied him. This was all he had to offer his God.

In the Bible, God was famous, as in the story of Cain and Abel, for being more pleased by living animals and their slaughter than by a basket of inanimate vegetables. She imagined a lamb struggling, its little hoofs beating against the slate, her father with one hand holding the frantic animal down and with the other slicing into its throat, blood spurting out, soaking the altar cloth, splattering his linen robes. Everyone would be relieved, grateful and happy to be alive. People would sense that someday they'd witness their own death but somehow still live.

The ushers returned to the back. One was holding out his hand, welcoming her to line up for communion. The wine would hit her empty stomach like a French kiss and besides, in her mind communion was a paltry and unsatisfying ritual, nothing compared to its precedent, the lush and drunken last supper, where disciples feasted on bowls of olives and roasted chicken and the bread was so delicious Jesus compared it to flesh. No, today she wouldn't go; better to eye the altar from here. She shook her head, but the lady next to her told her little boy she'd be right back and slipped past Ginger. The boy was leaning on a hymnal coloring a Sunday school sheet that read *God Made Me*. As the line grew she recognized only a few of the parishioners; frizzy-haired Jean Gephart, who was afraid of her dishwasher and fat Mrs. Clayton and her startled-looking husband Herman. There was Ann Heinz, the goody-goody girl in her floral dress with the lace collar and her exhausted alcoholic mother Barbara. Old Klass was here today too; he was the only member left from the old days. Most of the old Germans lived in row houses or garden apartments downtown; they hadn't taken to the new church building. Her father hired a van to go down and get them Sunday mornings, but the only one who ever came, sitting alone in the back, dreaming like a wizened duke, was old Klass. He was tiny now, less than five feet, and seemed smaller still in his three-piece suit. He kept cinnamon candies in his pockets for the children and was always calling himself a Prussian Lutheran and a libertine.

She watched her father raise his hand and make the sign of the cross to dismiss the first group of communicants. All rose with their heads bowed. The organist used the softer tones of the choir keys and only a few people sang.

> *Take my will, and make it thine / it shall be no longer mine /*
> *Take my heart, it is thine own / it shall be thy royal throne.*

Her father lifted his head and glanced at her. His features were not tense or angry, but Ginger knew what he wanted her to do. She stood with an irreverent swivel of her hips, loosened herself from the pew, and walked up the aisle to the far end of the communion rail, knelt down, watched from the side of her eye as he placed a wafer on each extended tongue. *This is his body given unto you for the forgiveness of sins.*

The real world should seem foreign and out of focus from inside here; a church was a way station between this material world and the next immaterial one. But she saw cars like meteors made of colored light zoom past on the highway. And heard a truck heave and honk, the driver hurling his load into the express lane.

He moved closer, smelling of nautical aftershave and dry toast. *This is his body given unto you for the forgiveness of sins.* He placed the wafer on her tongue and she brought it back into the wet cave of her mouth. The host stuck to the roof, tasted like typing paper, like white grade-school paste.

He began again with the silver chalice. *This is his blood shed for you.* He tipped the cup to a man's lips, then lifted it, cleaned that spot with a piece of white flannel. *This is his blood shed for you.* He was near. Flutter of robes, his muffled side step. She raised her head, took the cup's lip between her own, and looked into her father's face. Large pores were open and oily around his nose, and his eyes reflected pinpoint faces of parishioners in the first pews. *This is his blood shed for you.* The red wine stung her gums. She tried to swallow but a cramp punched into her abdomen. Flinching, her mouth opened and wine dribbled down her chin, spattering circles round and soft as berries on the wooden rail. *How ridiculous,* she thought, *that this is happening now.* He was already behind the altar, making the sign of the cross, touching his forehead, his heart, then each shoulder. "Go in peace," he solemnly said.

As she rose the muscles in her stomach contracted and she felt that monthly paradox, a light-headedness with unbearable bloody weight. She walked along the side aisle with her thighs clamped together so that no blood would drizzle down her legs. A man sat in the back row in a baby blue golf sweater silently moving his lips, not the wide-open shifts of singing, but whispering furtively to the trustee beside him.

She hurried out the narthex doors, down the stairs toward the basement, past rows of Sunday school rooms, the nursery. Posters lined the hallway, enlarged flowers with Bible verses printed underneath and a banner that proclaimed PEACE TO ALL WHO ENTER HERE in big, badly cut, felt letters. She swung open the door to the ladies' room and flipped on the light, pushed open the stall door, squatted back toward the toilet seat and reached under her skirt, pulling her pink cotton panties down. It was one of the bad pair with the loose elastic waistband and the pee-stained crotch. Now the material there was blood-soaked and heavy, smudges of red on the inside of her thighs. She sat on the cold toilet seat, listening to the last verse of the communion hymn.

> *Take my love; my Lord, I pour / At thy feet its treasure store /*
> *Take myself, and I will be / Ever, only, all for thee.*

At Christmas her doll Kimmie was always baby Jesus, and she was always an angel with a tin foil halo and cardboard wings. Sometimes she chewed on her long cuticles and said *The body of Ginger take and eat.* Once when she was still in her crib an angel had hovered in the corner of her room all night, and on Halloween she saw a demon squatting in the bare branches of the pear tree. She remembered the exact moment she'd first found out that the soul wasn't a real organ like one's heart or kidneys and the story her father told her about the little boy who wanted to get to heaven so bad he kept trying to ride his Big Wheel off the garage roof.

Organ notes caused the cork panels of the ceiling to tremble and she saw her father's long, elegant fingers gripping the base of the common cup and tipping it to one fearful face after another.

* * *

The convenience store reeked of steamed hot dogs and microwave burritos. She laid the box of tampons, the tiny bottle of Advil, and the Tall Boy beer on the counter and watched sweat gather on the fair hairs of the cashier's upper lip as he rang her up and put everything into a paper bag. She'd been in here a lot, but his round face was always expressionless. She asked for the bathroom key, watched him open a drawer, lift the plastic disc with the key dangling from a dirty shoelace and hand it to her, then swing back to the Slurpee machine where his *Playboy* waited.

The back of the store smelled of spoiled relish. In front of the bathroom door, a mop sat in a bucket of gray water. She squeezed between the Pepsi quarts stacked to the ceiling, flipped on the bulb that hung over the tilted medicine chest. Paneled with fake pine, SUCK ME was scratched into the wood with a car key. She couldn't get the warped door to close properly, set the useless key on the sink's ledge, and opened the box, quickly unwrapping a tampon. She pulled her panties down to her knees, squatted back over the toilet and pushed it up inside. Blood dabbed one end of the cardboard applicator like a lipstick-stained cigarette. She tossed it in the garbage, then stepped out of her stained panties, reached up to the dispenser and pulled out several brown paper towels, wrapped her underwear in them and stuck the bundle deep into the garbage pail. She aligned the arrows and pressed up the plastic Advil cap, peeled off the foil cover, and threw that and the cotton ball into the trash. Popping the beer, she put the can to her lips, dumped four or five pills onto her tongue and washed them down with a mouthful of beer.

In the mirror, little red pimples dotted her forehead and her eyes looked glazed like when she had a fever. The pills obliterated the pain, though nothing could counter the bee-buzz sensation, strong as a refrigerator's hum, that signaled the world on the verge of collapse. And during these days she had eagle-eye vision, so the bathroom revealed itself in painful detail, the hairs stuck to the porcelain bowl, the flecks of soap dried on the mirror, and her own features yearning and greasy.

She slipped the Advils and tampons into her blue suede purse and carried the beer out, then laid the key on the counter. The cashier stuck fresh hot dogs onto the metal prongs of the rotisserie. Balancing herself on a car, she stepped off the elevated cement and walked across the vast parking lot. The only time it felt right walking in a parking lot was to or from a car. Any other time it was humiliating, like being left behind at a party. Wild daisies and monkey flowers flourished alongside the road, the sky was static-gray and boring as a headache. Shredded plastic bags hung from the trees, rippling out like strips of ghost flesh. The Heinzes' Buick passed. Anna turned her head on Ginger and smirked, one of those stiff half-smiles that show a mixture of superiority and pity. Ginger felt her face get warm. There was nothing wrong with walking. People around here thought you were crazy if you didn't ride around in an automobile. Anyone on foot was considered immoral and insane, no different than the guy from the psyche center who escaped once a month in his bathrobe and slippers.

Jesus didn't have no automobile! Ah Jesus. Lover of little woodland animals, baby bunnies and little brown bears. Jesus, with those dreamy blue eyes, was the only person she'd ever known who'd been murdered and she knew his exquisite corpse by heart.

She wanted to start her own religion. Its premise would be simply that if you sensed someone needed kindness, you acted. If a homeless guy asked you for a dollar, instead of getting angry you'd just give it to him. You'd stop if a lady had a flat tire or if someone needed a ride. One of the symbols would be a hitchhiker's raised thumb. The communion ritual, the symbolic changing of a tire. She imagined herself in her father's robes going down on her knees into the roadside mud, turning a gold ratchet to loosen the nuts from a lame tire.

She saw skid marks reaching across the blue asphalt like charcoal strokes and found the brown blood flecking up now like dried mud, and the trail of trampled grass that led into the woods. She thought of going down and looking for the headless deer. But it'd be rotting already, covered with flies and squirming maggots. She crossed the street, walked a little faster in the roadside weeds because she felt it coming on strong now, not the pills but a vague uneasiness and longing. Ted was right when he said Sunday was the best day out of seven to get stoned. She'd go to his house, lie on his bed, watch the Sunday afternoon movie, split a six-pack with him. Maybe he'd sense how sad she was and do one of his little shows, sing the holy-holy-moly song or the one he made up as he went along, about how pretty she was and how much he loved her. Ted was fucked up, but he was still the only person who knew all the ways to make her feel alive.

Three: GINGER

Through the slow afternoon of fading light they lay on the soft fitted sheet's big oriental peonies, pale blue petals languid as any flower in an opium-soaked dream. The blue comforter wrinkled like water at the foot of the mattress. Conversation wandered as it always did toward Ted's favorite topic, the devil's physical manifestation in this world. She told him how she'd once seen a demon squatting in the branches of the pear tree outside her bedroom window. "His skin texture like a lizard covered with soot, his eyes slimy as a silverfish, and when the thing uncurled his tongue it looked like a thin black snake."

Ted's eyes were wide as he told how his father used to hang his terry cloth robe over the door that separated his room from his parents'. "At night, I'd hear footsteps, turn to look, and see the bathrobe transformed into a devil with a gray, bullet-shaped head. This devil tormented me every night, until one afternoon, while lying on my bed, I heard the devil's footsteps, felt it's breath against my cheek, but instead of being overcome with fear, I punched out at the demon. That was the last time the monster bothered me; after that, the robe was just material that reeked of cheap cologne and beer-soaked sweat."

Ginger looked at him, unsure if he was being sincere or mocking her; sometimes it seemed he just made up anything to stay part of the conversation.

"I rode over and checked out the deer head this morning," Ted said. "Its eyes have developed a milky film that makes it look blind."

Ginger felt a queasy riff in her stomach. "I bet that deer had been eating out of fast-food dumpsters," she said. "Bun crusts and hamburger gristle." She wondered if it's spirit might have passed into her. Ted made her close her eyes, try to visualize shifting leaf light, an appetite for tree bark and vernal grass, but all she heard was a dog whimpering in the apartment next door.

"That deer's trapped on my retina," she said.

"That's what ghosts are," Ted said, "spirits living inside of you. Your eye is like a movie projector, shining them out."

Ginger nodded. Her mother was often in her eye, thin, pale, and breastless, black stitches running in and out of the skin of her chest, not slanted and orderly like they had been, but going every which way, so she looked like a rag doll repaired haphazardly with black thread.

"Some people, like Jesus or Elvis, have souls so expansive," Ted said, "that when they die their spirits become a part of all cellular life. They coat the world like a fine membrane, distill into every atom, and that's why people see them inside redwood trees and on corn tortillas simmering in frying pans." This last idea excited him and he sat up against the wall; his pupils expanded as they tried to soak up the last bit of daylight. "It happened last year," he said. "I was at my grandma's house down in Bixler. She made TV dinners and we ate them on TV trays with cans of Coke on the porch. She was worried about the boy that mowed the lawn, said he was overcharging her, that when he came into her house to use the bathroom he stole things out of the medicine chest. She didn't like the way he was always spitting in the grass. She went on and on and I'm sitting there, starting to feel really uncomfortable, you know; I was getting that trapped-in-the-DNA-of-this-pitiful-family feeling; her paranoia, her TV trays, her shoe-box-size existence. So I went into the bathroom, locked myself in, opened the window, and lit a fat doobie. There was a white crochet doll with a plastic head over the spare toilet paper, a bowl of pastel soaps, frilly curtains, pink towels with little bears. The air started to hum, then I felt this pressure pushing up against the top of my skull, and I realized how wrong this bathroom was, how it didn't suit me, and then I looked at my face in the mirror and realized my body was just as wrong and external as this bathroom—how completely arbitrary it is that we're stuck in this body or that one—and that's when the pressure gave way and I felt like I was floating in water, like I do when I'm having a dream."

"How's that?" Ginger said.

"You know," he said, a little embarrassed now that the story was over, "all dreamy and shit." He pulled her onto his lap and kissed her, trying to keep the stretched skin away from her cheek, but Ginger still felt the hard line of his fleshless jawbone, and she had the sense she was kissing a skull. He moved his hand up her thigh and pressed his fingers between her legs, so he touched the tampon cord.

"Go take it out," he said. "I don't mind the blood."

She walked down the hallway, wearing only his long Black Sabbath T-shirt, her swollen breasts swaying with a lush animal grace. The half bottle of red wine she found in the refrigerator and the pills she took earlier, plus a few tokes off his joint, all combined to numb out the pain in her stomach and make her weak-kneed and very high. She liked pot; it gave her a giddy sense of possibility, even hope, like warm weather in early spring or getting an unexpected large amount of money. The conversation made her dizzy too. They'd been talking like this ever since that first night at the bar in the Quonset hut out on Highway 9. She liked his Prince Valiant haircut and how he sat alone at a back table sneering at the local band. When she asked him what he did, he laughed and said cynically, *Saving the world through prayer.* The conversation that followed was the best she'd ever had, how he loved the butter-soaked Texas toast at the Western Sizzler and the tiny Graceland at the miniature-golf course on Garfield Road. He was the first person to say the new post office as well as everything else out here was ugly and she was so grateful; a few hours later she went for a ride in his car and fucked him in the backseat.

Flipping on the bathroom light, she saw a water bug run over the white Formica and disappear behind the sink. Mold spores pock-marked the shower curtain, inched up the white tile walls. The toilet was shellacked with missed piss, hairs imbedded like ants stuck in amber. The room was humid, the walls swampy. Nature was taking it back. She sat on the toilet seat and reached between her legs, found the white string that hung out like a price tag, and pulled. The blood-ied mouse plopped into the water and sunk down moodily to the bottom of the bowl.

She walked down the hall with her legs pressed tight, paus-ing in the open doorway of Steve's room. Dusk's flaxen light flooded his unmade bed and the pentacle plaque hanging above it. There was a poster of Iron Maiden, one of Blackie Lawless drinking blood out of a human skull, and a huge movie poster of a slimy seven-headed demon, each face with red ember eyes and horns the length of yard-sticks. All his tapes, Krokus, Metallica, Judas Priest, were piled up by his boom box, and there was one of his pen-and-ink drawings taped up on the closet door, a surrealistic image of a saw-toothed demon with a butcher's knife in its throat and blood cascading down from its right ear into a basketball hoop, which became a spigot and flowed into a drinking glass. The caption read in big black letters: I GOT STONED AND I MISSED.

Steve worked during the week as a janitor at the hospital cleaning the operating room after surgery and, when he could get them, dealt acid and 'shrooms. Ginger felt a little afraid of him. It was easy to imagine the seven-faced dragon, between the bed and the Formica dresser, bobbing its multiple heads like thin-stemmed wild flowers frenzied in a breeze. She heard a rumor he'd poured gasoline over a dog and set it on fire and that he'd spent a year in jail for cocaine possession. Ted told her all his satanic stuff was just a joke, that none of the rumors were true. "Steve has been shitted on all his life," he said. "He's a great person, just totally misunderstood."

She walked down the hall into Ted's room, lay on the towel he spread over the sheets. A flutter of blood spilled out of her, trickled down the inside of her thighs. It always felt like more blood than it actually was. The body was weird that way, magnifying its mass and function in the mind. Ted sat on the edge of the bed. At his feet was a shoe box full of junk: screwdrivers, nails, plastic pieces from broken clocks, his old pot leaf belt buckle. He hunched over so all she could see was his bare back, his jeans so low the crack of his rear showed. The room was drenched in smoky twilight, white light glowed from his tape player. The music was over, but the blank tape played on, a silent hum as incomprehensible as snow falling.

Moisture ran into the crack of her rear as he spread the lips of her pussy and wet his pointer finger with blood, tugged up her T-shirt, so the material gathered in folds above her bra and touched her just under the tiny bow, pressed his finger into that hollow cleft at the top of her rib cage, then swung his hand down along the curving bone. His touch left a dark line, and sent out rings of sensation like a pebble tossed into water. Sliding his hand up higher under her shirt, his fingers were cold in a sexy way, like when you first take off your underwear and your bottom is bare against a cool vinyl car seat. Pushing her bra up, he cradled a tit away from her ribs. This gave a sudden sense of her own delicateness and she shuddered. Ted undid his jeans and pushed them down to his knees. Crouching over her, butt up, balls hanging, he leaned his head down and swayed his tongue messily into her mouth, jabbed his cock against her stomach, the red skin shifting around the hard inside part.

"You're so beautiful," he turned his head so that Ginger could see the scar that made the left side of his face unrecognizable. She saw nuance, shades of red and pink lush as tapestry in his mottled face. He pushed himself inside her, suspending himself over her. Long greasy strands of hair fell forward, shadowing his features; the silver cross around his neck swung just above her eyes. She helped herself along by thinking of the girl she'd seen in a porno magazine with a shaved pussy and then of certain parts in the Manson book, how during an acid trip Jesus said to Charlie, *These are your loves and you are their need.* How he'd gone out to the family bus, filled a pan of water and given himself a whore's bath, how when the girls came in he washed their dirty feet, one by one, how the girls in turn washed the feet of their boyfriends, and how suddenly the bus was filled with naked bodies. She saw Charlie balling one girl while finger fucking another. Ted rolled over so she could be on top, but she didn't press herself up, just clung to him. Sex was psychic. His cock inside her. Her cock inside him. Not boy. Not girl. Just frenzied protons in an electrified atom. She squinted her eyes so the light from the tape player looked like a quasar, like the big bang, like God making life out of nothing. The spirit of God hovered over the face of the water and she saw the smashed pomegranate, the figs swollen and split, honey dripping over everything. All the flesh inside her swelled with blood, tightened until it was hard to tell that they were separate. *Come into me,* she thought, and he did.

* * *

A few hours later Ginger woke and felt music vibrating the walls of the apartment. She rolled in the sheets to the edge of the bed, then stood and walked into the next room and sat on the floor next to Ted. The duplex living room was sparse; a TV sat on milk crates and Steve's bench press and free weights were pushed into one corner. Death metal riffs blasted so fierce she pressed her spine against the wall, afraid the boom box would crack and the speed metal dragon would burst out, scaly and blue-green as fish skin, its eyes slick as blood, breathing fire from its flaring nostrils, quoting from Revelations in the voice of a God gone bad. It was completely dark outside now, just some murky light in the oven illuminating the gray walls and silver racks, efficient and mysterious as a submarine trawling the kitchen floor. The rectangular window was smudged with meat juice, splattered with particles of petrified food. Dishes were piled high in the sink and a stack of pizza boxes and beer bottles surrounded the doorway. Carpet fibers pushed this way and that, like the coat of a mangy dog, and Ginger imagined them shifting languidly like seaweed caught in currents of windy water.

Steve walked into the room and knelt in front of her, held the plastic mask over her nose and mouth. It was the kind anesthesiologists used in surgery, the kind that gas came through to put you to sleep. He'd made this contraption with stuff stolen from the hospital supply room—a glass beaker with a heating nozzle, rubber hose. She watched him take a bud from the plastic baggy, load it into the copper bowl, and flick his lighter until the flame caught the dried leaves, singed them into red embers. Steve wore rings on every finger, a skull, a glass eye, a crucifix, and though he'd just showered, changed into jeans and a flannel shirt; his body odor hinted of blood.

"Suck up," he flicked the lighter. Steve was the only child of the county's most volatile couple. Sightings were mythic: the time they'd got drunk in the lounge of the airport Holiday Inn and knocked over the singer's synthesizer, the midnight screaming session in the parking lot of McDonald's, and the car accident, where Steve's mother had crashed into a green highway sign and was found unconscious in her baby-doll nightgown, an open bottle of white wine still locked between her legs.

Steve was legendary for his fights at high-school parties. One second everybody would be standing around sipping from 16-ounce plastic cups of keg beer and the next a strange fusion would go through the crowd and Steve would be going head-to-head in the mud with somebody who rubbed him the wrong way. It didn't matter what it was about; any reason was only a pretense—school loyalty, some half-drunk girl, something somebody said about his favorite band.

She took her hit and handed Ted the mask, but he appeared to be asleep, leaning against the wall with his eyes closed, his head tilted back. Steve took the mask from her, loaded the bowl again, and held it over his own nose and mouth; with his other hand he brought the fire to the green leaves. The flame spread an oval of orange light over Steve's features, which were as even and pleasing as a movie star's. His hair was slicked back, so that shiny cords spread like horns over the top of his head, and under his eyes the lavender skin was delicately veined as a flower. He took another hit, then put the rig beside him and lay out on the carpet with his hands folded behind his neck.

"Did you ever think about killing someone?" he asked.

Ginger looked over at Ted, who was stoned, sleeping, or both. "I could see if some guy fucked with me," Ginger said. "You know, raped my mother or killed my dog . . . but I wouldn't just go out and kill somebody at random. That's sick." Her voice was firm and reprimanding.

"It's just a hypothetical question," Steve said. "I know it's all a circus of shit."

The brown dog chained to a tree stump ran at them, raised up on its back legs, and started to bark. Its white teeth flashed in the dark and Ginger saw the furless pink skin of its tummy. Steve and Ted stood on the porch, shoulders hunched forward, hands curled deep inside their front pockets, both shivering. Their warm breath made puffs of frosty steam as Steve knocked again. They waited, listening for the TV or the hippies' footsteps. Ginger stood in back of them near a swayback lawn chair, picking leaves off a dead geranium in a coffee can. Christmas lights were strung around the little house, but most bulbs on the green wire were smashed or burnt out except a purple and two greens along the gutter and a red one looping down over the top of the door frame. She looked at the ruined garden, the skewed corn stalks, tomato plants reduced to wet heaps, each woven with a strip of stem-securing cloth. The green-pea vines had rotted into the white cord that held them, and the zucchini and squash decomposed to seeds alone. Only the cabbages would grow all winter, ugly as bottom suckers. Beyond the garden, through the thin plot of woods, she saw the lighted windows of Sugar Ridge floating in the branches.

"The fucker is always home," Steve said, turning to glance back at Ted's car parked next to the hippie's old Impala, then pounding harder with the side of his fist.

"Jesus," Ted said loudly, "you know he's in there."

"Let's go," Ginger said. "Maybe he doesn't want to see us."

The old hippie was usually nice. He once gave her tea for a sore throat made of slippery elm and cayenne pepper, but he was also an eccentric guy, swore he cured himself of cancer by eating only millet and tofu. Once he showed them how he'd sliced his finger, then stitched it up himself with a needle and thread. The hippie could be delusional too, talking about his CIA file, how he knew for a fact that the cartels had him on a hit list. Sometimes he'd speculate about future societies, after Armageddon, how the earth would be this utopian place with everybody living in tree houses and eating organic strawberries. Ted's connection to reality was fragile as a spider's web, and it wasn't good for him to be hanging around the hippie. Last time they were here, Ted told the hippie he was growing mushrooms in his room with purple grow lights and plastic trays of potting soil. And after that she'd heard him tell his mother he was going back to school. He even talked shit to her father, stuff about trying to help some poor kids who lived in the low-income housing out by Robert E. Lee Highway.

The frosted bulb over the door lit up and Ginger heard the dead bolt slide. The hippie pulled back the wooden door and opened the screen one.

"Goddamn it, Woodstock," he yelled at the dog. It whimpered, walked back to the cedar doghouse, and lay down on a muddy blanket. "Get on inside here," the hippie said, holding the screen door open. "Go on into the kitchen. I got a house guest sleeping in the living room."

A young girl was spread like butter over the couch, flushed with sleep, sweat pasting baby hairs to her forehead, an Indian tapestry thrown over her like a blanket, her breath so shallow and infrequent Ginger worried she was dead.

Ginger followed them through the living room into the kitchen. The hippie pointed to the wood table, then swung open the refrigerator and bent over to get some beers.

"What's with sleeping beauty?" Steve asked as they sat down in mismatched chairs. "Friend of yours?"

"Hell no!" the hippie said, carrying the green bottles of beer to the table and sitting down at the head. "She just showed up here this afternoon, said she'd heard about the old days and that I had drugs."

"She looks young," Ted said. "What did you give her?"

"Half a lude," the Hippie said. "I had to! You wouldn't believe how she went on, screaming and crying. Said she'd tell the police I was a drug dealer if I didn't give her something." He lifted the bottle and took a swig. "She's a freaky little chick, says she was at that camp with Sandy Patrick."

"No way," Steve said.

The hippie nodded. "She was talking about it right before she passed out."

Ginger tipped back her chair so she could see through the doorway into the living room. Long drugged breaths lifted the material of the girl's sweatshirt, showed her navel and smooth rounded belly glowing in the blue television light.

"How's the preacher's daughter?" the hippie asked.

Ginger let her chair fall forward, felt her face warm.

"Fine," she said.

"You should bring these pagans with you to church sometime." He lifted his beer in Steve's direction, his red braid shifting on his back and the good-luck medallion made of cherry seeds and red thread swaying over his leather vest.

The hippie was a real hippie. He'd once lived on a commune somewhere in Oregon, where he'd actually practiced free love and learned how to make both butter and cheese. He could bake wheat bread too and curdle yogurt. When they'd first met him he had a dozen chickens and a goat. He told great stories from the commune about snakes getting in the outdoor shower and about their leader, an eighty-year-old Canadian guy who sang the blues better than Muddy Waters.

"How's business?" Steve asked.

The hippie sat back and sighed. His lips were delicate and wet, exotic as a pink orchid against the coarse strands of his rust-colored beard. "It's getting scary." He pulled his braid over his shoulder. "The guy I usually buy from, the one with the hydroponics complex out on Route Seven, got tipped off that the Feds were onto him. He closed down and split to Vancouver. There was another operation out of Florida, run by a young kid, a Dead head," he rolled his eyes, "but I hate the risk of driving up the interstate, makes my ass sweat just thinking about it. These days," he shook his head, "nobody cares about the spirit, man, nobody wants to transcend. It's not just drugs folks are down on, but the whole spirit world. Hell, you can't even talk about God without people catching each other's eyes and thinking you're crazy. The fundamentalists have turned

Jesus into a redneck. It's pathetic. I think we should let the Indians take over the government; it's the only way to satisfy the earth. People think you can just build a mall or a highway, but the earth is not into that—you have to respect the earth, and if you don't the earth gets hungry and wants blood. That's what plane crashes are all about, blood payment. People think revolution is about intentional violence, but it can be so organic. No different than when those underground plates shift in an earthquake—it's like a new community forms beneath the old and then suddenly whoa," the hippie shook the table so Ginger had to put a hand down to secure her beer, "tremors start coming up, getting bigger and bigger, knocking down skyscrapers and highway ramps. Ginsberg man, he had it right, he said the first rule in any revolution is to keep a lot of vodka in the freezer. I seen him smoke joints rolled with twenty-dollar bills. One time we wanted Dylan to play at our rally and Allen, man, he says, *Dylan might play, but only if war is never mentioned, only if the protesters all carry signs with pictures of different kinds of vegetables.* But the best was Che; he was a God to us. Once we all went down to South America to see him. He comes in wearing his green army pants and his black felt beret, and he starts talking about the revolution in Cuba, the guns they got stored, and his plans for his people, and I was thinking, oh man, to be a real revolutionary with uniforms and guns, and then it's like Che read my mind, because he gets this real serious look on his face and he says, *I envy you. You are fighting in the belly of the beast.*"

The girl moaned and the hippie paused, glanced into the living room, and said, "Looks like that loony chick is waking up." He looked at Ginger. "Go in there and sit with her. I don't want her freaking out again."

Ginger pushed back her chair and walked into the living room, sat on the arm of the couch. Bunches of dried roses hung from the ceiling and the room reeked of pot smoke and gingery Middle Eastern perfumes. In its clutter, the place reminded Ginger of her own house, the same ambiguity to the world of things. On the TV was a washed-out African plain, then close-ups of zebras turning their heads in quick gestures of fear.

The girl yawned and moved her hands over her head, stretched, so her ribs pressed through her skin and the tiny bones in her neck cracked. It was a gesture so private in its animal intensity that Ginger felt embarrassed. The girl opened her eyes to slits, tried to focus first on Ginger, then the darkened window over the TV.

"What time is it?" she asked.

"Around eleven," Ginger said.

The girl nodded sleepily, looked at the TV. A herd of gazelles ran across the screen. "What's your name?"

"Ginger."

"I knew a girl once named Pepper. There were three sisters and they were all named after spices." The girl sat up and pulled her sweatshirt down.

Ted came into the room. "We're going in a minute." He sat on the other arm of the couch. "What's on?"

"Some nature show," Ginger said.

The girl stared at Ted. "What happened to your face?" she asked him.

"It got blown off in Nam," he said.

The girl looked at Ginger and then at Ted.

"You look young for your age," she said.

"Yeah," Ted said, "I'm kind of magical that way."

"Don't tease her," Ginger said.

"It's okay," the girl smiled. "I know he's only joking."

The hippie asked Ted to take the girl home and so she sat now in the backseat, legs folded under her and the army blanket pulled over her shoulders. She had a baby doll's voice and knew all the words to every song on the radio.

"Don't you wish," the girl said, "that you could move things around with your mind, so you could get a Coke from the fridge by just thinking about it. Wouldn't that be cool?" She tapped Ginger's arm like a child wanting a response from its mother and said again, "Don't you think that would be cool?"

Ginger turned her head and smiled and the girl took this as affirmation and leaned up over the front seat. "You know," she said, "last night I had a dream that a witch flew out my bedroom window with my doll, and my mother had to call the army to get it back."

Steve gave a condescending snort and Ted glanced at her with a look that said *Stop encouraging that girl*. But Ginger liked her, knew she was talking so much because she was lonely, that she needed some attention.

"I don't feel so good," the girl said suddenly. She was offended by Ted's and Steve's patronizing silence and slumped back heavily against the seat to pout.

Ginger turned around, "Are you going to be sick?"

The girl shook her head, tightened her lips, and leaned her

cheek against the window. She was trying to be brave, the way little girls do when they've scraped their knee or have a splinter, when a bumblebee's wiggled into their frilly anklet and stuck its stinger into the pink flesh of their soles.

"So where are we going?" Steve asked. At first he couldn't keep his eyes off the girl's tiny breasts, but her talking had ruined all that and now he just wanted her out of the car.

"I live in Woodbridge Hills," the girl said, "right up there." She clung to the door handle, her breath making little clouded circles that she wiped away with her sleeve.

Ted made a left turn off the road into a pre-fab subdivision hugging the highway. The entrance was marked with a well-lit billboard surrounded by white gravel. Streets were named after the contractor's daughters: Ashley Court, Jennifer Street, and Laura Lane.

A lot of women were abandoned here, left to raise teenagers in exhausted-looking split-levels. Mothers who were at work, or at the club, or so tired in the evening they didn't care what happened. Some slept all weekend with their doors locked; some went out to the Hilton Bar and drank margaritas. Inside these houses, the TV was always on and kids jumped on the beds until the slats broke and had wrestling competitions in the basement. Walls were smudged with food and toothpaste and she'd even seen muddy tennis-shoe tracks on the ceiling, as if divorce had made the children light as feathers.

"Go slow," the girl said, as they passed a blue ranch house. Inside its bay window, a table lamp underlit ceramic comedy and tragedy masks mounted over the couch. "That one," the girl said, pointing to a white split-level, with burgundy shutters and a colonial eagle hung over the door. "That's it," the girl said, "that's Sandy's house."

The silver Tot Finder sticker drew Ginger's eye to the second-floor window, and deep inside the room a votive candle burned on a white dresser. Next to the dresser was the painted door Ginger'd seen in the newspaper; the white unicorn, the rainbow, the fluffy clouds, all painted in a sweet amateurish style by Sandy herself.

"Is anyone in there?" Steve asked.

"Her mother," the girl said. "Her father lives in a different state with some other woman."

The light went on in the second-floor window. Beyond the sheer curtains Ginger could see the edge of a double bed and a long, low chest with a portable TV on top. The curtain floated up and the round anxious face of a woman hovered there in the dark pane of glass.

"Shit," Steve said. "Let's get the fuck out of here."

Ted skidded up the road. The girl started to cry and said that Sandy was the nicest girl, that there was always something kind of sad about her, that sometimes she wore the same skirt all week and her tops and bottoms didn't always match and sometimes too, when she was nervous, she stuttered. "God," the girl screamed, "I can't stand it!"

There was no fire, just glowing embers giving off a hazy orange light, though it was still easy to see the deer's head balanced on top of the TV. Ted had dragged the TV from the dump and set it up at the edge of the fire. All the knobs were missing and the screen was smashed out. Inside, a metal board with Japanese writing and a lattice of multicolored wires snaked this way and that. He carved a hole into the top of the deer's head with his jackknife and stuck in a red flare, kept for emergencies in the trunk of his car. The pink flame was low now, directly above the fur, like a Pentecostal fire. Ginger was thinking the deer was the last one left and there was no doubt it did have an apocalyptic look, the way wax spilled onto the fur and thickened blood dripped over the edges of the television. But the thought was crazy; there were thousands of deer, maybe millions.

While the others had taken the flashlight and gone to look for more firewood, Ginger went out to pee around back in the safe spot of feather moss and butter fern, where she'd never seen a snake and there was no poison ivy. She walked down the pressed-dirt path, past the sumac grove and the dead cat in the open box, its skeleton delicate as a chalk math problem. In the woods she lifted her skirt and squatted, listened to the sound of her urine hitting leaves, then walked to where a cushionless couch was set up around a cold campfire. Burnt Bud cans. Blackened angles of wood. The low-lying mist clung to the weeds, made her feel dreamy, and she threw herself down on a safe-looking patch of grass and thought of the deer, how it hovered above the hood in the sliver of sky between the dark tree line on either side of the road. It was the earth's spinning that made it seem to pause and float.

An airplane's red lights divided the splatter of stars and she could feel the bright eyes of angels in the icy constellations and sense a sort of second-place grace spreading over her. Wind rocked the leaves, made her shiver and curl up sideways with an ear to the earth. There was the rumbling of the highway, but then behind her what sounded like a footstep, a crackle of dry leaves; a twig snapped. She

Darcey Steinke

pushed herself up into a monkey squat, turned toward the barn,
thought of yelling for Ted. But if she spoke the devil would come
after her, fierce as a rabid bat. If he was watching her now, there
were a hundred places he could hide. She felt the thick lips of her
pussy still flushed and filled with blood.

Four: SANDY

A strip of light, radiant as a fluorescent tube, shone up from under the closed door, illuminating the edge of the bare mattress, her bound ankles, pale blood-starved feet, the toenails like lavender shells. Millions of dust particles swirled around, made her feel like a tiny figure inside a glass dome, where the miniature scene never changes and specks of white plastic careen around sublime as real snow.

The cat raised its sleepy head, looked with indifference toward the door, then, satisfied no one was coming down the hall, shifted its belly and walked over her, hip to rib to shoulder bone, as if these were raised rocks and her flesh a riverbed. Crouching, it tongued her ear, with sly little strokes that resounded roughly through the cartilage. Sometimes the cat chewed her hair, and at first, before she learned to keep her eyes shut, it had batted her lashes as if they were spiders.

She listened to the rain behind the boarded window, the TV downstairs, and for any sound of his presence among these. The laugh track rose and fell and she heard him hack, clear the petal of phlegm from his throat, shift his weight on the couch. She sensed his anticipation, obvious and uncomfortable as summertime humidity. It was nearly time, and she needed to let the seconds build to minutes, the minutes to hours, listening to the fly trapped inside the ceiling fixture buzz hysterically against the glass.

He stood, took one step, then another. She pressed her ear to the mattress, felt the muscles in her neck harden and separate. The steps varied in cadence from carpet to wood to bathroom tiles, then stopped. She heard the stream of his pee, first hard, then softer until he flushed and the water swirled down the drain. He jiggled the handle until the tank started to fill up. Drops of urine flooded her vagina; pee trickled between her legs, puddling in the crack of her rear, then soaked through the fabric of her nightgown into the bare mattress. The smell of urine tightened her stomach muscles, stretched her nightgown up like a tent between her hip bones. She struggled to wiggle her butt off the damp spot. *It was okay,* she said to herself, *it didn't really mean anything. I am still the same person.* She tried to move again, but each time, the cord that ran under the mattress forced her back into the cold pee.

Somewhere downstairs a washing machine rattled to life, must be from the little room, off the kitchen, the one her mother called the mud room, where a table, covered with detergent gran-

ules and single socks, stood across from the Maytags. There was a
shopping bag overflowing with puffs of blue dryer lint and a freezer
filled with frozen hamburger meat. Her mother had put in a late
load and she tried to separate the sound of the engine from the
thumping cadence of wet clothes. She was lying in her bedroom
half asleep, listening to the rotating water downstairs and to the
music box on her nightstand, watching the ballerina twirl around
slowly. She called her Elena, a name she thought Russian and so-
phisticated. The dancer was the size of her pinkie, with a tiny brown
bun, pink toe shoes, and a little satin skirt that covered the top of
her white legs. Her stuffed animals, that napped all day on the
yellow gingham pillow, were displaced now, strewn into the alley-
way between her bed and the wall. Each one had a name, a per-
sonality all its own, but in the dark it was only their eyes, toxic
green or red, that shone up at her and made each seem like tiny
sinister strangers.

She felt the blueprint of her house around her, a phantom
sensation, hard to throw off because she wasn't in her own bedroom,
but held hostage in this room with its wood-paneled walls, brown
boxes stacked in one corner and a colonial chair. This room could
be anywhere, maybe in one of the Main Street mansions downtown.
She'd always thought of them, white or butter-colored with round
turrets and generous front porches, as somewhat ominous. Most had
turned into boardinghouses, the big rooms cheaply remodeled into
drywall apartments, where dazed-looking people in sleeveless
T-shirts and cheap vinyl shoes sat all day long looking out the window.
Or maybe it was one of those ratty condominiums out by the airport. A boy at school told her prostitutes and drug dealers lived there.
Once she heard the big globular sound of a water cooler and figured

she was being held in one of the half-empty glass office buildings along the highway. Other times she thought she'd been pulled through a portal into another dimension, that this room was underground, that the man with the white beard was the devil and this her particular hell.

She turned her ear to the wall, heard the static snap of the television obeying the remote and turning itself off, the electricity slithering out of the TV, through the cord, and back into the wall. He threw his weight up, the couch springs adjusted, and he walked like a younger man, an altogether different man, into the kitchen. He broke the vacuum of the refrigerator and felt around inside. She heard glass jars clink, the rustle of aluminum foil against the wire shelf. A fat hum kicked in as the fridge spilled cold air into the kitchen and began to generate more. The door sucked shut and she heard his hip nudge a chair, the squeak of its legs on the linoleum. He opened the microwave, closed it, his fingers pushing buttons; the familair beeping sounds rang out, then the electric drone as water molecules heated up in whatever he'd decided to eat. He turned on the kitchen faucet; water rushed through the pipe in the wall next to her bed, gave off a slight aura of damp humidity. The heat released old smells trapped in the paint: hair spray and stale smoke. The microwave beeped its electronic alarm, and water pounded against the porcelain, until her ears rang and her throat dried out. Panic spread down her torso into her pelvis, snaked out through her limbs. Her fingers felt thick and numb and her mind folded back in half, into quarters, until it became tiny as an origami bird made from delicate silver paper. She thought of flesh flushed with moving blood, and then of dead flesh, blue-gray and puffy. When you had a sore throat or bumped yourself and got a bad bruise, that was what rotting would be like, but you wouldn't feel it happening because you'd be dead. And it wasn't until she said the word, put her tongue to the roof of her mouth, and forced the air up from her lungs, that she started to struggle.

The door swung open, a pillar of hall light spread against the wall, the cat jumped up and ran through his legs; then the light was gone and he flicked on the flashlight, waved it once across the room. It veined his beard orange, showed his fish-scale eyes, and made the yarns of the carpet look shiny and magical, as if you could wish on them for love or winning money. Squatting, he set the can of food on the carpet, leaned the flashlight against the wall, and moved over her, unlatched the metal hook from the cord around her wrists and the strap from her ankles. Sinking his fingers under her armpits, he yanked her up against the wall, unpeeled the tape from her mouth, and picked up the can, took the spoon—always the same tarnished silver one with the fancy filigree handle—from his shirt pocket, and dipped it into the beef stew. It was the same always, soft carrots, potatoes, translucent onions, bits of grayish meat in a room-temperature gravy.

Each spoonful was too big and he never gave enough time between them to chew. He never spoke either, just went about his duties like a good-natured but bored nurse. A lump of stew fell onto the smocking of her nightgown. He used the spoon to scrape the gravy and stringy meat up and put it back into her mouth. In the twin panes of his glasses, she saw the girl with the short black hair. She watched the shifting jaw, the mouth purse, wrinkle, then open up again like a baby bird's. And while she felt the chilled spoon on her lip and the food fragmenting around her teeth, still there had to be some sort of mistake.

When the can was empty he set it aside, slid one hand under her thigh and the other just below her shoulder, and carried her into the bathroom, placed her on the toilet seat. Stepping back, he waited to hear tinkles of urine or blobs of poop. She saw the tiny green dots of his big wristwatch, the glowing second hand twitching from one dot to the next like a tiny frantic bee. The textured shower stall picked up a little flashlight and sparkled like frosted glass. She made water noises, first a waterfall, then stream water over rocks, then the 'piss piss piss' her mother had made when she was being potty trained.

"Oh for Christ's sake," he said, yanking her wrist and heaving her over his shoulder.

When she was scared at night her mother would come into her room and sit at the edge of her bed and say *Think of something nice.* She would always envision the violets that grew on the shady side of the house.

He laid her down, took the afghan from the bottom of the bed, and covered the line of light under the door. There were pink roses and arrogant red ones. She heard the tiny teeth of his zipper disconnecting one after another and then a sound like when skin hits water in a belly flop, and her elbows skidded forward, burned on the polyester mattress. Her forehead bumped the wall hard. Lilacs were beautiful, so beautiful, and she went right down into the center of that tiny flower, to the stamen, to the pistol, to where the yellow pollen brushed off on your eyelashes and the smell made you drunk with love.

* * *

He'd stripped off her nightgown, flipped the pee-soaked mattress and given her his shirt. The material reeked of aftershave and sweat and she felt like he'd swallowed her whole, that her body floated in his dark stomach along with lumps of chewed-up chicken in a lake full of beer.

The cat curled around her head like a voluptuous wig. She felt its damp breath in her ear, its wet nose snuggled under her earlobe. She'd lain here through a myriad of untenable days and nights, one distinguishable from the other, only in the slightest rise of light. The afternoon sun illuminated the wood grain of the boarded-over window and sent out a smell of chemically processed pine, so she could see the bug corpses lying prone in the light fixture and that the decals on the headboard were Power Rangers and Ninja Turtle Warriors.

At first she'd kept track of each day by assigning it to an object, the three brown boxes in the corner of the room, the chair, the light fixture, the mattress itself. After each object was invested with a day, she'd look to the ceiling and count off one swirl of textured paint after another. It worked for a while, but a string of dark rainy days confused her and she had to give it up; all she knew now was feeding time, feeling it in the hollow of her bones as she listened for his footsteps on the carpeted stairs.

The TV talked in hushed tones of love and betrayal, of suspicion and remorse. Heat pushed up from a vent in the corner, made her sleepy, and she thought, as she often did in an effort to figure out how she got here, of all the things she'd ever done wrong. Her mother was upstairs making the beds and her little brother sat on the couch in the living room looking at his picture books. She felt reckless, threw herself against the cushions, and began to brood. She'd

overheard her parents arguing and this gave her an uneasy and for-
bidding feeling; everything seemed impermanent and annoying. Clear
snot ran under her brother's nose and drool stuck to his chin. He
read his book in baby talk, his voice rising and falling, and when he
turned the pages to a picture of a silly-looking rabbit with long ears,
he looked at her and said, "Cat."

"It's a rabbit, stupid," she'd said, pushing him off the couch
so he banged against the sharp edge of the coffee table and then fell
onto the floor. As he got up she'd noticed how his arm hung funny,
how he pressed it to his side. And while that was probably the worst,
it wasn't the only mean thing she'd ever done to him. He was so gull-
ible. She'd give him an olive and say it was a sweet grape or tell him
about the Christmas before he was born, when she'd gotten a unicorn and a baby bear.

He was older now and she couldn't fool him, so she'd get
the upper hand by making fun of his friends, saying they were stupid,
that a girl would be crazy to go out with them, that they were ugly,
greasy-haired nerds who picked boogers from their noses and ate
them. Once she'd gone on for so long his face got red, his eyes teared,
and he ran from the room, though he usually just tried to joke it off.
He was nice to look at, with his pink skin and somber black eyes, his
hair always cut a little too short. He had a smell too, tennis shoe
rubber and grass.

Her eyes got warm, then wet, and she felt tears dribble out
the sides, down into her hair. If she could see him now, she'd put
one hand on each of his shoulders, look directly into his eyes, and
confess all of her sins, say she loved him too, though it was risky;
she'd never said it before and he might get embarrassed and run out
of the house, jump on his bike. *Come lie on my bed,* she'd say to him.

He liked science fiction books and she'd read out loud, like she used to when they were little and it was raining or snowing and she had nothing else to do.

Her father played his bluegrass records two states over, but she could hear the melody if the wind was right. Her brother talked nonsense on the cordless phone and Mrs. Bailey, the English teacher, told her no one would ever take her seriously if she didn't learn to spell. A burglar came up through the toilet and she heard the Gestapo banging on the door. Her flesh covered his ottoman, so his feet could be cozy by the fire. He untied her, wrapped her in the afghan, and carried her down the hall, through one dark room after another. The furniture stood around like bad ideas. The metal mesh of a screen door pressed against her thigh, then flapped behind her. She saw her pale hand dangling down against the blue and sparkly asphalt; it seemed so far away *how would she ever get it back*. The cool night air brushed against the bottom of her feet and she realized with a shock that she was *outside*.

The cat was not with her, probably prowling for deaf birds and blind mice out in the world. Many times she'd tried to push her own soul into the cat, so that when the man came in, she could run past him and squeeze out the kitchen window. The TV was on downstairs and hot air blew up through the floor vent. But then the mattress tipped and the floor pitched sideways, and she recognized the hum of an engine and the sound of wheels bumping up out of a pothole. She tipped her head back, saw stars beyond the front seat glimmering through the windshield, the Big Dipper to be exact, huge and glamorous like the movie version of a geometry problem. She looked at his neck, found the red birthmark at the base of his skull, and knew he was driving her somewhere else in the van again. The radio played a song so soft and incomprehensible it seemed like a ballad sung from the bottom of the sea.

Heat flowed over her, strong as smoke. Rolling up on her side, she wiggled her shoulder so the ratty afghan fell away, and she saw that her chest was bare and that she had on a diaper, the disposable kind, and that the odd sensation of wadded paper and moisture meant that the crotch was already wet. She looked down at her bare chest; except for the slightest swelling around her nipples she was, as the boys said, flat.

He glanced at her in the rearview mirror, in a perfunctory sort of way that made Sandy think she'd been sleeping for a long time, that he thought of her as any other cargo, boxed televisions, or field-grown potatoes. The sky outside the windshield was turning from black to electric blue. Dawn was her favorite time. Even at home after a long night of hearing strange sounds and linking each to an intruder, it was only with the first hint of light that she could go down deeply into the smoky kingdom of sleep.

Inside the sleeping bag, she pulled her knees into her chest and listened for what Robin would say next. It was around 8:30, almost dark; through the flannel weave she could see the girls had their flashlights on, were using them to look at magazines or paint their toenails. Sweat rose on her face and behind her knees, and she was grateful for the cool air tinged with pine and the smell of river water that came through the big screen windows as it started to rain. Drops slapped the late summer leaves and bounced across the canvas roof. The cabin was clean like a cave, well swept, but with moss growing on the window ledge and all sorts of tiny bugs crawling up and down the walls.

"Have you gotten the curse?" Robin asked. She was the meanest girl at camp, wore her hair long with little wings flaring out like steak knives. She had breasts and fresh hickeys on her neck and a story about how she and some high-school boy got drunk on rum and Cokes.

Sandy's only answer was a little moan to prove she was unconscious.

"She thinks tampons are to put up your butt," Robin pointed. All the girls laughed and Sandy felt her mind dissolve into the rapids near the little waterfall where the girls weren't supposed to go. Ghost snakes of white water slithered into one another, then vanished. Her father pounded on the bathroom door and begged her mother to come out; her brother came into her bed and at first they just looked at each other, rolled their eyes, and tried not to laugh, but then her brother put his hands over his face and started to cry. She knew there was something wrong, that she sometimes smelled like pee and couldn't seem to pick out clothes that looked right together. Robin put her foot on Sandy's head, jiggled it so she bit her tongue.

"Leave me alone," she said, straightening her back and shooting out of the sleeping bag.

Robin stood above her with one hand on her hip. "All right," she said, "you big fucking baby."

* * *

Sandy stood at the edge of the clearing, under the branches of scrub pine and red maple, away from the other campers, watching the first of the floating candles round the bend in the river. She moved up the path; the girls were still singing the camp song, about sisterhood and the splendors of nature.

Pausing on the steps of the cabin, she watched the little flames attached to bark boats blink through the leaves of the trees, moving like a Milky Way into deeper darkness, away from the lights of the camp. Inside, she hunched over and took off her clothes, the shy way, as if all the girls were already there, pulled her flannel nightgown over her head. It was embarrassing because all the other girls slept in oversized T-shirts.

She shimmied down into her sleeping bag and tried not to be afraid. The day had been a long one, moving, as they did every day, from canoeing to archery, from swimming to modern dance. She'd felt nauseous and thought every minute of calling her mother. During arts and crafts she started to cry and ran down to the latrine before anybody noticed.

She pressed the skin low on her stomach and remembered she'd forgotten to pee. It was the fruit punch at dinner and the can of Diet Coke she'd gotten from the machine afterward. The girls moved up the paths and Sandy knew there was no time to dress again and go to the latrine, so she jumped up and ran outside, walked barefoot along the edge of the cabin until she found the spot of shadowed moss, pulled up her nightgown, and squatted, leaning back so the urine wouldn't bank in the arches of her feet.

Way back in the woods she heard a breeze blow back the

leaves and rattle the branches, and as she finished and stood, someone gripped her arm and jerked her toward the woods. She thought
it was Robin, who'd been waiting all day, narrow-eyed and mean,
to get her alone and beat the shit out of her, but the figure was thick
in the chest; maybe it was the stable boy or one of the guys that
worked in the kitchen, maybe they'd noticed how sad she was and
decided to save her life.

Blackberry briars caught on her nightgown, pulled until the
cloth strained and snagged; her bare feet hit sharp rocks and broken
sticks and strange thorny plants. He yanked her so fast it seemed like
her legs would fly up and she'd float diagonally in back of him. She
felt rain on her face and started to cry. He turned his head, his features better defined now in the opening of trees, in the sublunary
light. His face was round with a long white beard and yellow teeth.
Sandy recognized him as the lonely troll in fairy tales. Her head got
swimmy and her knees dissolved and he scooped her up and carried
her deeper into the forest.

Sagging burlap grazed the tip of her nose; the coarse threads
tickled and she squinched her features and sneezed, soaked her flannel bit with saliva. Not that it wasn't already wet, her tongue rim-
ming around its velvety nuance, until she knew its sinews as well as
the geography of her own teeth. The mysterious smell of lust and
loneliness seeped through the hotel mattress into the musty box
spring. The powerful scent shrunk her tiny as a figurine left under a
doll house bed. He wouldn't need the van now; he could carry her

in a velvet flute case, or in his pocket, like a Barbie doll, her tiny toes brushing his leather belt, her head resting against a copper penny warmed by his groin.

Like a searchlight turning figure eights over the highway, she beamed her need out, so the numb drivers in their cars would flash to a girl in a diaper tied diagonally under a motel bed. But even if it worked, they'd just shake their heads, dismiss the image as a half-remembered scene from a bad B movie, assume their mind had lost its way with fatigue and was wandering places it shouldn't.

Her stomach quivered. He hadn't fed her for several days, just a couple swallowfuls of warm Coke. Maybe he'd bring her back some food; anything would do, a package of chowder crackers or an old candy bar. She wanted french fries, the thin kind, sweet and delicate. Saliva gathered between her gums and cheek.

At the beginning of summer, before camp, she lay out in her bathing suit in the backyard, reading and daydreaming, mostly about the boy she'd gone into the closet with during a game of Seven Minutes in Heaven. She'd expected a pretend kiss, but once the door closed he pressed into her with such longing she thought she'd faint. In the hottest hour of the afternoon, the bedding flowers wilted and the sun electrified her dream of a bare-chested boy in white satin basketball shorts lying among her stuffed animals, the pink rabbit with the bow tie, the downy yellow duck. She'd heard her glass of Coke tip over, opened her eyes to a deer's thick tongue licking spilled soda out of the grass, antlers covered with fine white hairs and its eyes dark as corn syrup. A dog barked and the deer jerked its head up, stood perfectly still, then ran back into the woods, its white tail moving as expressively as a face. She'd gone into the house and got lettuce from the refrigerator, spread it out on a gray stump just inside the tree line. The deer came back that day and nearly every other, slowly beginning to rely on the fetid produce. Even now it probably lingered during the day in the woods between her backyard and the highway and at night stepped right up to the sliding glass doors.

That wasn't the only strange omen. A few days before camp, she'd gotten bored, put a few stale hamburger buns in a zip-lock bag, and walked along the highway guardrail to the park. Mosquitoes hovered like static electricity and the air was so thick with humidity it was hard to breathe. A woman with blonde hair was reading a romance novel and smoking at one of the picnic tables. Her chubby baby lay nearby on a blanket spread out on the grass, wearing only a diaper, its hair wet with sweat. Sandy asked her how old the baby was and the woman said *two* without even lifting her eyes from the page. Its head was too big, its eyes dull and unfocused. There was something wrong with the baby; it was sick or retarded. She'd walked quickly around the small man-made lake, the dirt path dusted with downy feathers, toward the wooden dock. Opening her bag, she took out the bottom half of a bun and threw it into the water. Mallards swam over to her, but before they got near a huge black carp surfaced, took the bread in its mucusy mouth, and swam backward until she could no longer see its shape in the muddy water.

Shadowed legs of chairs, the heating panel, the haywire shag carpet might as well be seaweed, rusty cans, and silt-covered stuff found on the bottom of the lake. She pointed her toes, pretending to wind across the room, belly grazing the carpet, her movements as easy and unhampered as air.

Back and forth she flipped her wrists until the pins and needles came and then the warm rush of blood. She listened, cars on the highway, a distant TV, and the sweet smell emanating from a spot near the nightstand where someone once tipped over a can of beer. She released her bladder and let pee soak the paper crotch of her diaper. It was hot at first and sort of comforting, but then it turned cool. She shivered, felt goose bumps raise up on the backs of her arms.

Listening to the motel door shut, to one link rattling against the next as he secured the chain, she flattened her cheek on the carpet, watched his disembodied shoes move, as if enchanted, around the edge of the bed. He clicked on the TV, the screen lit up the bedspread fringe. He walked to the nightstand between the two double beds where the push-button phone and the ugly glass lamp sat silent and the gold Gideon's Bible lay unopened in the drawer below. His toes wilted up like a piece of burnt paper and the frame rocked as he leaned his weight onto the bed, lifted the spread, and poked his head underneath. She saw the white beard strands at the corner of his lips and the whites of his eyes magnified behind the thick lenses of his glasses. He untied the cord around her wrists, swung down to her ankles, then patted her leg to signal she should shimmy out. Sitting up between the two beds she pulled down the gag; it hung around her neck like a wet bandanna.

He threw a T-shirt into her lap and she put it on, sat up on the bed; a brown paper bag stood next to the phone.

"Go ahead," he said. "Open it."

She lifted out the plastic spoon, the wax paper baggy of soy sauce and fortune cookies, then the warm white carton, and undid the flaps. Thin strips of beef and red pepper floated in a brown curry sauce. He stared at her, as if she'd cast a spell over him.

"You like it?" he asked, and when she looked up to nod, his eyes were wild and grateful as a stray dog's and she realized all this was happening because he was very drunk.

One spoonful followed another. She ate as fast as she could, afraid the food would be ripped away. The curry was strong, with lots of gooey gravy. When it was gone, she ran her finger along the sides of the carton, then licked the warm sauce from the tips.

Still he stared at her with his fishy eyes. He reached across and put his hand on her bare knee. She looked at the hairy knuckles, the sapphire ring. He was dressed in a colorless shirt made of thick white cotton and a pair of khakis.

She asked if he was going to tie her up again. Things were so much more certain that way. His expression, which she'd catalogued as hopeful, even friendly, turned sharp and he smiled stiffly, called her a stupid bitch, and with the heel of his shoe he kicked out at her. She was so surprised she lost her balance and fell off the bed. Quickly she righted herself, crawled underneath the bedspread, but he grabbed her by the ankle and yanked so her face slammed into the nylon carpet and he flung himself down, strode her chest, like she'd do to her brother when she'd won a fight. He pinned her hands under his knees as she bucked up a few times, arched her back, tried to get him off, but the troll just smiled, reached around for his wallet. It was Western style, with roses stamped into the leather. He flipped it open, took out a piece of paper, and unfolded it. His birth certificate, worn fuzzy on the edges, the typed information fading out.

"See," he held it up to her, "it doesn't matter whether you have a girlfriend or not." Sandy felt herself trembling. It was worse than she thought. The man was completely insane.

He got off her. Sandy felt her chest expand with air.

"Stand up." He yanked her up, his hands on her hips, then tripped her down onto the bed. With one hand he clenched the pee-heavy diaper so the tapes broke, and he threw it against the nightstand, where it fell wet and lumpy behind the bed. Brown sauce spurted up her throat and the sun flared out; tendrils of fire ignited the clouds, violet and bloody blue-red. Fire fell like rain, the trees hissed and smoldered, branches full of dry leaves flared up. If she let him do it this time, the whole world would come to an end. Using the muscles in her upper legs and her knees to push off, she lunged forward and out of his palms' grip. Her hand was on the chain, the other twisting the doorknob, and she was out. The sweet humid air tasted of car exhaust; white lights and red ones blurred on the elevated highway. Pebbles stuck to the pads of her feet and the asphalt grated her skin; the cement supports were too tall to scale so she ran up the exit ramp and tried to wave down a car on the interstate.

Five: GINGER

It wasn't so bad in here since she'd brought a lamp from home, one of the colonial ones from the basement. Now the cement walls of the church office and her mother's huge green metal desk glowed as if the room were continuously held in the glittering palm of God. She pulled out the bottom drawer. It was filled with old stuff: an ancient jar of fountain-pen ink, colored pencils, a blue ball of rubber bands, a booklet of baby Jesus stickers and a plastic container of gold stars. Yellowed business cards with antiquated lettering were scattered on the bottom. Her mother used the stars to distinguish particularly good Sunday school drawings: the divine doves of adolescent girls or the bloody pictures the older boys drew of Jesus on the cross.

She thought of the old church downtown: plywood nailed over the cracked stained glass and red graffiti tags sprayed over the fieldstone. Stuffed animals dangled from the bushes and trees outside: teddy bears caked with dirt, some missing eyes, and a few naked dolls, noosed like tiny babies with disconcertingly cheerful expressions and hacked-off hair. Across the street, the X-rated theater looked on with sly mastery. Before the church was vacated, crack heads forced open the back door and stole the antique silver communion chalice. The fiends, as her father referred to them, left a dead rat on the altar and with red lipstick wrote *fuck you* in the margin of the big leather Bible. Together they spent several days cleaning up. Her father used a broom to push the furry body across the marble, over the altar's edge into a paper bag. With a damp washcloth she'd wiped away the swear words, leaving a blotchy red stain over most of the Book of Isaiah. Mulhoffer had been smug about the break-in; her father was crestfallen and contrite. He still hoped to convince the congregation to keep the old building, turn it into a soup kitchen or a shelter for homeless men.

She peeled the label off a wax paper computer strip and stuck it onto a flier that reminded parishioners membership photos would be taken in two weeks. Already she'd folded and stapled hundreds of them and was almost done with the labels. Encoded in the names was secret information, confided by her father to her about people in the parish. Mrs. Hofner, who told everyone her husband died of a heart attack, had actually nudged an electric radio into his hot bath; or the Koenigs, whose eldest son hung himself in the backyard wearing his sister's prom dress and the Robertson newlyweds, who got involved with cocaine and kinky sex and were still in a detox center in West Virginia. Then there were the more mundane confessions, the loneliness of the older members, the disappointments of middle-aged ones. Sometimes her father saw people in his home office and Ginger would put her ear to the door, listen to a woman complain about her wayward husband and a mother tell how she'd forced her teenage daughter onto the pill.

Her father was away on Monday making sick calls. First he did the shut-ins, the handful of elderly Germans living in apartments downtown. He sometimes joked about the thick smell of sauerkraut embedded in their forties-style furniture and their knickknacks on pine shelves: dogs and elfish children in lederhosen. He always spent a full hour with Mrs. Mueller, who used to be the most powerful member of the church before Mulhoffer. She donated the money to buy the organ and made a special contribution every summer so the vacation Bible school kids could go to Holyland USA. Mrs. Mueller's grandfather started the glove factory, world famous for making long, elegant evening gloves of silk and satin and short pastel day gloves with pearl wrist buttons. Germans who fled the Third Reich were offered jobs in the factory, and this was how the church downtown got started. Though bedridden, Mrs. Mueller, a formidable lady responsible for both the expansion of the library and the new community theater building, still lived in an old Victorian on Main Street with a middle-aged nurse and a gardener who puttered around the lawn. Every visit Ginger's father gave her communion; he opened his black leather traveling case with the blue velvet indentations for the decanter of wine, the small chalice, a round tin that held the wafers stamped with lambs. He kept a lightweight tippet in his coat pocket, gold crosses embroidered on either end. Draping it around his neck, solemn as a melancholy magician, he offered up the cup to Mrs. Mueller's thrush-covered tongue, her white hair so thin that as she bowed her head, he could see blue veins through the translucent skin of her scalp.

Next he went to the Lutheran Home and held a lunchtime service. Organized in the makeshift chapel, a piece of red felt was thrown over a card table below a gold cross made by a resident out of Popsicle sticks. In wheelchairs and walkers they came, expressions ranging from reverence to resolve. Finally he ended the day with a drive over to the hospital, where he'd visit anyone the nurses said needed help. Last week he saw a boy whose face had been messed up in a fireworks accident and a woman who gave birth to a blind baby. He always looked in on the man with the goiter growing out of his neck and the diabetic woman who'd had her legs amputated just below the knees.

He wouldn't be back until late afternoon, so Ginger could afford to take a little break before batching the fliers. She opened the newspaper and spread it over her desk. That redneck councilman was rallying strong voter support for his theme-park proposal, stating that it would bring thousands of much-needed jobs into the area, and the woman with terminal breast cancer settled her case out of court with the electric company. Company spokesperson Lisa White, conceding that a settlement was necessary to curb bad publicity, continued to deny that power lines have any relationship to cancer. On the religion page, "If the Deerpath Creek mega-church were a business, you can bet people would be clamoring to pick up some shares of its stock," an article began. Buried near the back by the movie ads was a police drawing of a man with a beard and in small caps: POLICE MAY HAVE BREAK IN PATRICK CASE.

On Saturday at approximately 1:00 A.M. police reported that a motorist driving south on Route 15 saw a young woman run across the Motel-8 parking lot toward the highway. "I couldn't believe my eyes," the woman said, "because the girl was naked as a jaybird."

Mrs. Alper from Valdosta, Georgia, was returning from a visit with her sister in Lynchburg, Virginia, when she saw the young woman sprint across the motel parking lot. Because of the angle of the highway, Mrs. Alper lost sight of the girl and only spotted her again in her rearview mirror. "She must have fallen because there was a man with a beard lifting her off the ground." Alper didn't report what she saw until the next morning. "I had to convince myself I hadn't fallen asleep and dreamt it," she said.

Local officials searched the hotel but no one fitting Alper's description was in residence. Mr. John Winslow, the night clerk, reported a man fitting the description had checked in alone the day before. When asked about the man's disappearance, Winslow responded that it wasn't particularly odd. "To avoid highway congestion and the heat, many people get early starts."

Police detective Bret McMullan, who's been handling the case from the beginning, says there is no way of knowing if the girl was Sandy

Patrick. "For all we know, Mrs. Alper may have witnessed a domestic spat." Nevertheless, McMullan told reporters they would follow up all leads.

Patrick's mother, who is on leave from her job teaching kindergarten at Oak Grove Elementary School, says she's praying for the safe return of her daughter. "I know I'll see Sandy again," Ruth Patrick said. "I just know she's coming home."

Ginger remembered Ruth Patrick's face in the window, her frosted hair pulled back into a pony tail, the Chinese neckline of her bathrobe exposing her pale throat. She wished she could will Sandy home, make her materialize on the lawn and hover toward the door. But Ginger saw Sandy lying in the woods, her hair pasted to her head with dew and spidery vermilion veins starting to fester like splattered blood on snow. Red ants crawled into her nostrils, along the bottom rows of lashes and between her parted purple lips.

The church was drenched in tawdry, multicolored light. Rich washes of red and yellow soaked the walls and long green angles of light fell over the front pews and red carpet. In the old church the altar's guild—a handful of serious, middle-aged ladies, all with a reverence for good silver and table linens—took down the altar clothes and stored each ceremoniously in a carved cedar chest. But since the move to the new building, the women used plastic covers that Mrs. Mulhoffer ordered from a church catalogue, slipped them over the fabric on the altar, the pulpit, and the baptismal font so everything was dust proof and hermetically sealed.

Behind the altar was the sacristy, a little kitchen with a sink and spigot, a bar of new soap beside a dried-up sponge. Cabinets above and below were the same poppy red color as the countertop and though she never turned them on, overhead there was a row of fluorescent lights. She set the box of fliers on the counter near the silver-tone tray of tiny individual communion glasses. Each held one sip of wine. The trustees said in winter everyone got the same cold and that they wanted to replace the common cup with this tray of plastic glasses, but Ginger knew they suspected that Mark Rutland was gay. A few times she'd seen him with a thin man resting on a cane by the waterfall in the mall. To the trustees, AIDS was just another bad curse come to them from the city, like crack and high taxes.

She opened the cabinet over the sink where the long wax paper containers of unblessed wafers lay in rows like Ritz crackers. When she was little she'd found a whole pack in the backseat of her father's car and eaten every one. Alongside the wafers stood bottles of Manischewitz grape wine. Downtown, homeless men drank Manischewitz in wrinkled brown bags. On Sundays, the wafers on the sterling plate and the wine in the medieval-style goblet took on aura and import, became what they called holy, but backstage their glamour was diminished, no more important now than saltine crackers and Boone's Farm wine. Holiness was like that, you could never trap it or examine its uncanny elements.

She liked the old church better, but knew no place was really any more holy than any other. Once at Christmas, she went with her father to visit the old man who lived in a tin shack behind Mulhoffer's factory. Beside his bed hung a paint-by-numbers picture of Christ, a dirty silk scarf, and a gold dime-store locket that he said held a curl of his sister's hair. She took down a bottle, her hand hot on the cool curve of glass, and broke the seal, unscrewed the top, and drank, one mouthful, then another, until she could feel the fermented liquid warming her stomach, edging out the dull ache of her cramps.

If her father's office was locked, she'd leave the box of fliers in the Bible study room where the trustees counted money after the service. Her father told her a good Sunday was when every adult gave twenty dollars and the wealthy ones forty. Then he could pay the mortgage on the new building, his own salary, hers, the organist's, and buy supplies for Sunday school and communion, then put some money into a savings account for the computer, the new hymnals, and a swing set the ladies' guild wanted for the Sunday school children.

As she turned the knob, the door opened and she walked into the office toward his desk. Rudolph Mueller had acquired the set of stoic mahogany office furniture at the same time as the stolen common cup. Carved along the bottom of the desk was a chain of roses and the bookshelves were buttressed and bridled like a cathedral. Every shelf was filled with books by obscure German theologians, their names embossed in gold on cracked leather bindings. On the walls were two portraits of beloved former ministers. One was of Reverend Dunheinzer, who, along with his angelic wife, started the church. He'd been famous for his commonsense sermons and his love of flowers and small children. The other, painted in a photo-realistic style, was of a minister who'd had the church in the '50s, an overweight man with the fat face of a butcher. Fellowship was his forte and Klass told how in those days social events went on in the church basement almost every night. There was no portrait of the minister who owned a speedboat and had an affair with the organist, or the young man from Wisconsin who told so many lies he had to put his head in the oven and gas himself. Because the room was only half as big as the downtown office, with low ceilings made of corkboard, the furniture looked as if a crazy man had piled up file cabinets and bookcases, barricaded the door in fear of intruders or the great flood. The desk lamp showed a messy pile of yellow legal pads with her father's handwriting scribbled all the way down the pages. Her eyes continued to adjust in the murky light. His robes, both the cream-colored linen he'd worn yesterday and the sashes for Advent and Lent, lay scattered in a heap by the side of his desk. Hairs stood up on the back of her neck as the material shifted; gathers of cloth split and fell to one side and her father leaned up, his robes falling around him.

His face, which was usually taut and ruddy as a pilgrim, was pockmarked and lined from pressing into the ceremonial robes. The outline of a dove branded his cheek and the braided pattern of brocade indented one temple.

"Goodness," he said, "I fell asleep."

"Are you sick?" She assumed he came in late last night and left before her this morning, but she could tell by his beard stubble that he'd been here all night.

"No, no," he said jumping up, lifting the robes onto the leather wingback chair where he began hanging each on a wooden hanger. His long-fingered hands trembled as he smoothed out the materials. "Did you see those hillbillies from Deerpath Creek sitting in the back pews yesterday? They talked throughout my sermon and held their hands up during the closing hymn." A stole slipped off the hanger and he stooped over to retrieve it. "This is not a tent revival,

where toothless cowboys handle rattlesnakes and people run out of
their seats to be healed by some charlatan. What would Luther say?
He wouldn't like it," her father calmed himself, "though ultimately
it is his fault. With his fat hand he swept the virgin mother, all the
saints, anything exotic and mysterious, right into the trash can. If
only he hadn't made it clear that before God everyone who's been
baptized is equal, if he hadn't turned God's rituals into a commu-
nist meeting of brothers, into a circle of *friends,* then there'd be no
personal savior, no *born again.*" He said these last words with pro-
found disgust. "But it's not all Luther's fault. There was that horrible old hippie Karlstadt, with his imminent apocalypse and his
low church love-ins." His robes hung now, he walked wearily to
the leather chair and fell into it, moodily unlatching his clerical
collar.

"The trustees came yesterday with several requests. They
want me to cancel Klass's minibus. It's not economically viable according to them, and they want me to be more sensitive to the
entertainment side of the service. Deerpath Creek has four thousand
members and they said if we'd liven things up, use more modern
church music, get a drummer and a couple of ladies who can really
sing, we'd get more people and they'd be willing to give more too."
Her father was clearly disgusted. "They even went so far as to ask
for aerobics classes in the basement." He looked at her, his lips wet
with saliva, and in his eyes she could see already what he was about
to say next. "They even had the gall to tell me you're a bad example
for the girls in the parish. They don't like how you dress and that
you're seen with that boy. They call him a satanist."

"Write a letter to the synod," Ginger said. "Tell them this
place is going corporate and that you want another parish."

"No," he said, "I can't do that anymore. I'm getting too old. I'm not smart enough to teach at the seminary and not slick enough for the big-city churches. If I leave here, it'll be to some tiny ten-pew church in the middle of nowhere. Besides, Mulhoffer's talking about pulling out of the synod anyway."

"So are you saying that I'm fired?"

"Of course not," her father said. "Just be more discreet, and try to clean up a little before church, wash your hair, maybe put on a little lipstick."

"Mulhoffer wants me to wear lipstick?" Ginger's voice went up high.

"I'm sorry," he said, "but he does."

Steve pulled the match across the sandpaper, threw it side-arm toward the greasy lake. There was something careless and decadent about the curve of his arm. She figured he'd done this before, figured he'd done about everything in this town one could do to get in trouble. Like a firefly the match arched above the oil-soaked weeds and settled on the gunky surface. The tiny flame quavered as it burnt down the cardboard, then flared up blue violet before squatting down again, moving forward on the water like the spirit of a snake.

Ted had his arms around her; she pressed her back into his chest. Retribution was his idea and he held on to her so she'd know he'd take care of her, protect her the best he could.

"Hell yeah!" Steve yelled. "I told you the fucker would burn." His voice echoed off Mulhoffer's factory, which stood darkly in

back of them. Surrounded by barbwire fences, a few big trucks sat
in the back lot, but Ginger knew Mulhoffer would be too cheap to
hire a night guard or even buy a German shepherd.

Cement blocks were stacked near the pond, as were tin
canisters. Across the field of fool's wheat and wild daisies was the
back of Spring Run condominiums, Fox Ridge to the left, and on
the other side, through the thin woods, a strip mall that sold only
wholesale stuff, hair dresser supplies, and foreign engine parts.
Steve pitched matches; some landed in the weeds and went out
but a few sat on the surface like red water bugs before igniting,
flaring up in tawdry greens and yellows, colors usually reserved
for slutty eye shadow.

Steve told them how a baby had been born dead at the hospital that day, that the doctor went crazy trying to get its lungs
cleaned out. It was blue and the fetal monitor showed straight lines
for several minutes, but then it made a little noise. Its eyes shot open
and the damn thing screamed bloody murder. "That," Steve said, "is
what's known as risen from the dead." Ted said one of his mother's
friends had died on the operating table, saw white light, and a silver
cross floating out of her stomach. But then the smell of ammonia,
had forced her back to earth. And he'd heard about another case in
North Carolina where a man had died and they put him in a coffin,
but on the way to the graveyard he started knocking on the lid.
Turned out God sent him back because he hadn't had time for his
last confession and he had a serious sin against him, adultery or
murder, Ted couldn't remember which.

"Christ rose from the dead," Ginger said. "That's the only
person I know who's ever done it."

"Yeah," Steve said, "now everybody wants to do it." He

twisted his last match off and struck it, but this one he let burn down until it singed his thumbnail, turned the tip black. Ginger watched the snake move along the furthest basement wall, then slide into the fiery lake. Every Christmas, after she said Happy Holidays, showed off her Christmas dress—usually red or green velvet with a lace collar—her father sent her down into the Mulhoffers' basement to watch the toy train while he sat upstairs in the living room, thanking them over and over for their generous Christmas check.

The train moved along the wall like a black snake, slithered out of Ruby Mountain, where tiny elves wearing red caps and kneesocks picked at the rock all night long. The engine's headlights splayed over leafless wintertime trees and banks of plastic snow. Cargo cars filled with red plastic chips, underlit by tiny hobby bulbs, looked like embers, like crimson jellyfish. The elves lifted their hats, leaned on their shovels, and waved. One danced around the lake, a crazy skipping jig, while he waved his arms and talked to himself. Wind moved in the trees, put out the creeping chemical fires, and smoke rose like swaying spirits from the surface of the lake.

Ted wedged his car between two dumpsters at the back of Orchard Brook Mall. The backstairs reeked of cigarette smoke and boredom, of canned macaroni and Diet Cokes. In the dark, the snack machine gleamed and the soft drink dispenser hummed incessantly. Ted brought along the army blanket to spread over the new couches in case they decided to fuck and locked the department store door from the inside so they wouldn't need to worry about the janitor.

In the furniture department, he led her to his favorite model room with the big green velour couch and the matching leather wingback chairs. The lamp shades were printed with tiny British manor houses and there were paintings on the walls of men in red riding jackets atop horses, chasing foxes, leaping over stone walls. Books bound in leather, their pages epoxied shut, sat on wooden shelves and near the green plastic plant was a photo book on the history of Kensington Palace. There were a slew of other knick-knacks, a faux brass trumpet, horse figurines, one of a man with bagpipes and a kilt. There was a crest paperweight, not any specific family, just the generic kind women wore on T-shirts and middle-aged men on the pockets of their cotton sweaters. The place was dressed up for role-playing, all part of the same crazy Disneyland idea, suburban bathrooms transmuted into rural country stores and living rooms, like this one, into exclusive British men's clubs. Still, she liked the smell of all this new stuff, as intoxicating as gasoline fumes or pot smoke.

"You can hang out here and watch television, while I do my security guard thing," he said.

The idea didn't really appeal to her, but she nodded just the same. He wouldn't have to leave for an hour and maybe by then she'd get used to the room, could think of this place like a house put together in a dream, where you walk from your childhood bedroom into your father's office to the rec room where you lost your virginity. Ted turned on the televison and kicked his feet up on the coffee table. They watched a late-night mystery show where little girls ran backward because they saw angels. Their mother said one of them had levitated out of her bed and the other suddenly spoke perfect Latin. The second half told how a man tape-recorded the voice of his dead daughter threaded around the barking of a stray dog. The dog was white with pink eyes and sat regally on a dirty twin-size mattress in a trash-filled lot in Puerto Rico.

"Maybe that's why I always feel so weird and not really like myself," he motioned to the TV.

"What do you mean?" Ginger asked. He was always talking about mystical shit, but if you didn't rein him in a little, Ted sometimes satellited out around the farthest planet and headed for deep space.

"It's like that night," he said, shaking his head. "Everything was totally fucked up. You know the feeling; we've talked about it before. Somehow you sense that you're already dead." He shifted in his chair. "I was drinking beers, making macaroni and cheese, but I turned up the heat too high and fried the fuck out of it. I burnt my hand on the pan's handle and got pissed off, felt myself building into a rage, so I took a ride in the car to chill out. Just started driving around, kind of cruising different spots, the way we did in high school, over to Pizza Hut, past the mall, down to the dump, out to the lake, back to the high-school parking lot, then around again. I started to get this feeling like I didn't exist, like I was invisible, so I drove back to the apartment. Steve was at work and it seemed like nobody lived there. The place looked all empty and shit, just a bunch of junk pushed against the walls. I went into Steve's room and got his gun from under the mattress. The weight in my lap steadied me. I drove into the 7-Eleven parking lot and sat for a long time, watching people go in and out, watching the fat guy working the cash register. I realized I was thinking about robbing the place so I started the car and got back on the highway. My hands were shaking. It was fucking cold and all I had was my jean jacket. Eventually I pulled off the highway onto that gravel road that leads down to the railroad yard and just sat there with the gun on the seat beside me. Then all of a sudden I felt good, sort of light-headed and thrilled, and I knew what I was going to do. I was going to end it all and so I put the gun to my cheek and even then it seemed like a joke, and I remembered I smiled at myself in the rearview mirror and then pulled the trigger. There was a great shatter of glass and next thing I knew, warm stuff was all over my neck and I felt really muzzy, but it was nice, really really high like I was weightless and my head was filled with light and I was floating, thinking how this time I'd really fucked up, then wondering who this poor guy was with blood on his shirt. Then I ran my tongue along my cheek and I felt the hole, the open air on the other side. I looked at the dark houses spread over the hills and I felt cold; my breath was thick as smoke, and that's when I passed out."

"Sounds like you were almost dead."

"Yeah," Ted said, taking Ginger's hand, kissing her fingers, thin skin of his lips sticking to the ovals of her fingertips. "It was like a demon had a hold of me and I had to shoot myself to get him out."

She slipped her body under Ted's arm and put her head on his chest. He'd made it back. She admired that. His heartbeat and warm skin lulled her and she thought she might sleep.

"Gin," he said, moving her hair off her forehead, "I've been thinking about getting married."

Ginger kept her eyes closed and laughed, "Not to me."

Immediately his ribs came out of his chest like iron bars and he was Mr. Skeleton. She moved to the other side of the couch and he stood up looking down at her. "What's so funny about it?"

"Nothing," Ginger said. "I just thought you were kidding."

"I didn't realize you considered me so beneath you," he said grimacing, turning an awkward second toward the light of the TV.

"You know I'm totally into you," Ginger said.

"I don't need this patronizing bullshit." He walked toward the doorway that led into a girl's model bedroom.

"Ted!" she reached for his hand. "Don't be like this."

He shrugged her off and walked toward the canopy bed. The room was pink and white and delicate as a wedding cake. The carpet seashell pink and the wallpaper a mosaic of rosebuds, all the furniture was white, and on the dresser sat a silver jewelry tray and a tiny ceramic box with a doe-eyed figure of a shy little girl standing on top.

"I can't stand this shit," he motioned first to the room they were in, the white shelves filled with Nancy Drew books and pink ceramic kittens and angels with yellow hair and tiny glittering wings. Then he swung his arm up, to include the corkboard ceiling and all the other model rooms in a maze around them. "All this," he waved his arm showing he meant the whole store, "the mall, the highway, all the shitty stores along it, this whole fucking town and everyone in it. Fuck all of you," he screamed. Then with both hands he grabbed the lamp with the lacy shade and smashed it against the foot post of the canopy. Bits of bulb glass flew out like ice chips, and she covered her head; Ted pulled the wall mirror down, so it shattered, shards falling onto the bed.

"Ted, don't do this," she said. "I'm sorry, okay."

"Yeah, right, you're sorry. Fuck you!" he said as he kicked down the shelves, so the books tumbled and the cheap pressboard cracked. Then pausing, swaying like a drunk, breathing heavily, he unzipped his pants, pulled his cock out, and pissed on the princess bed with the thick pink comforter and the satin pillows with pastel floral prints. She staggered into the next room away from the flat wet sound, toward a zebra-skin bedspread and the plastic jade plant, and scanned the ceiling for shadows of the red exit sign. Through the next doorway, she ran by a chrome-framed poster of Michael Jordan, team logos all over the little-boy bed. Behind her Ted broke kittens and angels, one after another the smack of hollow ceramics turning instantaneously to gray dust. Out of the labyrinth onto the department-store floor, Ginger passed a wall of dead TVs and a wire basket full of soccer balls, then the long hallway, beating back the bathrooms, the employee lounge; she threw all her weight against the exit door and flew down the cement stairwell, till she was finally outside, running now across the asphalt parking lot.

She was far away from the mall now, past the bank with the drive-in cash machine, across from Chi-Chi's, the Mexican place were the suits came for margaritas after their long day under fluorescent light. She passed Wendy's and Burger King, almost to McDonald's. The big glass fronts were postered with drink and burger specials. Each chain had its own long empty parking lot separated from each other by barriers of cement. Humidity glowed under the highway lights. Gray moths beat themselves against the textured glass, the asphalt glittering below.

Ted wanted to bash things up, break windows, do wheelies, burn rubber until his skull cracked open and he fell down dead. Before the accident he was less bones than liquid, as if his thin frame were filled with water and his face smooth and beautiful as a child's. But memories from before the accident, precious as a fairy tale, were just as unreliable.

She heard the sputtering engine of Ted's car, the pebble rattling in his hub cap, and without looking back ran down the slope into the woods. There was a path that led into the Millers' backyard and across the road to Brandy Lane, where her house sat dark and silent, but she'd have to pass the deer. The woods were littered with Coke cans, empty cigarette packages, the aluminum and plastic catching what was left of the highway's white light.

What happened to Sandy was the worst thing that could happen to anyone. She remembered her only in fragments shown on television, the video of her posing at her dance recital, wearing an off-the-shoulder canary-yellow leotard with black sequins around the neck and a big black feather coming out of her hair, her face made up with rouge, mascara, and eye shadow. But when she tried to think of her now, it was always like a porno movie, a little girl with her nightgown pulled over her head.

Ginger hurried through the thin-trunked trees and thorny underbrush, but then paused. She saw something scurring away, disappearing into the weeds. The deer's body was badly bloated. Where the skin had been pink and furless, it was now yellow with burry blue veins running this way and that. She covered her mouth and nose, turned her head, the flies congregating in the ridges of raw flesh.

She heard another sound, maybe a dog wandering melancholy among the trees or Ted coming toward her. She moved around the deer, broke off the path, and slipped into the woods. A branch snapped in her face and her cheek stung; brambles pulled at her shirt. She panicked, felt her body lunge toward the backyards, the swing sets, the Weber grills, the cement patios and their sharp overhead lights. Her foot caught in a ridge of mud and she ran forward, leaving her tennis shoe. She ran toward the cul-de-sac lights, the deer chasing her, running like a man up on two feet.

Six: SANDY

Early light seeped through the green plastic bags taped over the window, making the room feel like the bottom of a swamp. Algae bled into the walls, spread over her mattress, oozed into her pores until she was green all the way through. Lying in muck, silverfish swam over her and an alligator crept past. Light intensified behind the plastic as if God were on the other side. She knew from books that children sometimes found passageways to kingdoms in the backs of wardrobes or by rubbing lucky coins. Maybe a boy wearing kneesocks and thick glasses would step through the plastic, blinking in confusion, because the moment before he'd been on the beach examining a piece of blue glass.

In horror movies, the portals that led to hell had gatekeepers, huge three-headed dogs, or blind men with tiny snakes living inside the sockets of their eyes. And if you went down into hell to retrieve somebody you'd better bring an ivory cross or a lock of baby's hair, because the devil tricked people, turned them into other things like bats or lawn chairs.

This room was smaller than the last one, her mattress a twin, and there was just a broken-down director's chair in one corner and a stack of newspapers in the other. She couldn't read where they were from, but by the layout, length, and spacing of the tiny letters on the edges, she figured they were in English. This comforted her, as she was afraid he'd taken her all the way to Mexico, through Latin America, where she heard men roamed in packs like stray dogs and killed tourists for their Visa cards and traveler's checks. Towns back in the rain forest of Costa Rica, where whorehouses had cement gates and barbed wire. If you ended up there, Robin had told them at camp, you'd never escape.

Oh-u. Oh-u. A bird called in a voice resonant with worry. *Oh-u. Oh-u.* But she couldn't answer through the gag, just thought of the bird's purple feathers, its pale peach beak and pink tongue, how all day it ate iridescent blue beetles and licked water off white flower petals. When he came in to feed her, pea soup right out of a red and white Campbell's can, he wouldn't make eye contact, and since she'd tried to escape he hadn't even touched her. It was a silent fight like her parents used to have. For days her mother wouldn't get dressed and rushed around in her nightgown acting crazy and officious. Her father sat on the edges of the furniture as if he were a houseguest. But now the man wanted to make up. All night the TV crackled and whispered like a campfire as he sat at the kitchen table writing, cutting letters out of magazines with scissors and pasting them to a blank page. Maybe the letter was to his mother or to an old girlfriend or some company whose product pissed him off; maybe he was working on a project, or filling out a work application. Or maybe he got an idea for a kid's book about a lonely troll that kidnapped a little girl right out of her subdivision. But she knew from the frenetic pace of his work, from the long meditative pauses where he went inside himself, that it was an important letter, that he was careful with the details. His scribbling went on for hours, cutting and pasting. He never looked at her once and for a moment she wondered if he'd forgotten all about her.

The gecko came up from where it lived between the wall and her mattress and stood frozen, lashing its tongue in the air. Its beaded head scooped the quilted material for centipedes and red ants. The movement of her eyelashes frightened the shy thing and it dived back over the mattress's edge. If Sandy sat very still in a forest filled with every kind of wild flower, chipmunks and squirrels would come up to take nuts from her fingers and lay their tiny warm heads against her thigh. She heard the turtle plodding along in the underbrush, eating soft leaves and meaty mushroom caps, the baby bear with a velvet bow tie listening patiently while the caterpillar, in his top hat, gave a speech in the style of Abraham Lincoln, talking mostly about Divine Providence but sometimes about Divine Intervention.

* * *

Sun baked the house. Like bread in the oven, she felt her mushy insides changing into a substance both dry and white. She was thirsty for water, for grape juice, for Sprite with crushed ice in super-sized wax cups, for a cold piece of watermelon, for a teacup full of homemade lemonade. And there was water and lots of it somewhere behind the plastic, a green lime quarry, or a man-made lake, maybe even an ocean. She heard the wet slap against sand and rocks and mud, and she pushed her tongue against the black electrical tape and for an instant hallucinated sucking on an ice cube, sitting in a baby pool, drinking from a cold can of Coke.

It was cute how her brother, when he was little, leaned against her legs, how he'd go around to the neighbor's front lawns eating the stale bread thrown out for the birds. Sometimes he'd take off all his clothes and run naked around the house. He was a preoccupied little kid. Once she asked what he was thinking and he said, "The big bang theory," and threw himself onto the couch. Another time he found a baby rabbit in the garage and squeezed its stomach so hard blood gushed out of its nose. The frog he'd found in the back woods had an orange belly and crazy eyes. He'd caught a catfish in the graveyard pond. Its skin was like black rubber and he'd pulled its whiskers off on the asphalt driveway, cut its heart out with an old hunting knife. The heart looked like a piece of wet gravel and her brother skewered it on the tip of the blade and carried it into the house.

She'd watched from behind the peonies, deciding to punish him, to take his little red race car and hide it under the mulberry bush. Winter rains turned to hard ice and encased the tiny automobile;

snow covered it like white frosting on a Danish. She stared at the
dream car swerving left, the expression of the Italian driver confi-
dent and intense. *Oh-u? Oh-u? Oh-u?* The bird had attracted others
and they were having a meeting, deciding how best to get her out.
The blue jays, who thought of themselves more like marines than civil
servants, wanted to bust the window, lead her out through the shards
of splintered glass. The egret, a coy international spy, wanted to
infiltrate the house solo, pin the man to his chair with its long lancelike
beak, while all the other birds flew down the hall, pecked through
the plywood door, and set the girl free. A flock of seagulls wanted
to tear the man's eyes out, then send the water rats in to finish him
off. There were other proposals, the robin's call for peaceful nego-
tiations, the owl's for covert night maneuvers. Sandy listened until
everyone started to talk at once, and the black crow said that there
wasn't much time left and shook lemons from the tree to get everyone's attention back to the matter at hand. But what was time to
her? A jewel beetle made its way across the ceiling like a floating
emerald. The faucet pondered a melody of drips. The shy gecko
stalked a fringy centipede. He was time, time was his heartbeat, time
was his breath.

"Fourscore and seven years ago," the caterpillar began, "all
beings were dedicated to the universal notion that every animal
is created equal. We were highly resolved in those days to the
proposition that the dead did not die in vain, but for the greater
good of these woods. That was when," the caterpillar swayed his

body to the right with whiplike rhetorical force, "this place was divine."

"It still is," said the bear, who had an optimistic disposition and didn't like anyone running down his home. He yawned, slumped against the tree stump. His bow tie was crooked, his hair matted with leaf bits and broken twigs, and he looked as if he were recovering from another drunken night.

"Don't interrupt," the caterpillar said, trying to look as large and dignified as possible. He gave a speech every day, but could tell that this was going to be a particularly good one. "It is for us, the animated, to be devoted to the work which they who fought on this hallowed ground here have so honorably advanced. For instance, we had in those days a family of fairies who could make a delicious casserole, using nothing but butternuts and tree bark."

"I'm glad they're gone," said the bear, yawning more dramatically, hoping the caterpillar would get the message. All the other animals had already gotten bored and wandered off; only the bear was polite enough to listen. He had a bad reputation, as a rogue and a dandy, but his manners were exquisite. "That fairy, the one who made rose petal slippers, she was a horrible gossip."

"Shut up!" shouted the caterpillar. "You're making me forget what I'm saying." He glanced down at his crib notes, etched onto an acorn beside him. "Whenever, if ever, we admit we are created by the four winds, our souls shall not perish from this earth."

"Amen," said the bear. "Is that it?"

"Yes," said the caterpillar stiffly. "I got all fouled up because of your constant interjections."

"It was a nice speech," the bear said, "but I'm too tired to hear you practice it again."

"Well I just might, and it'll be all your fault!" the caterpillar screamed. He was already mad at the bear for drinking the last bottle of champagne. "It's because of you that we need to raise money."

"We could sell lemonade," said the bear hopefully, "or paint some rocks? We could make seashell necklaces or weave pot holders, sell driftwood or the tail feathers birds drop onto the ground. I'll collect aluminum cans—they're all over the place—or I could give kindergarten students rides on my back. We could pick blackberries and sell them at a stand on the highway! I'll make floral arrangements out of foxglove and milkweed. I bet they'd bring a pretty penny. I think I'm old enough now to baby-sit, to feed children Rice Krispies squares out of Tupperware containers and referee while the little boys wrestle. I'd be good to the little girls too, read them stories about unicorns and princes, about trolls with bad teeth and white hair. . . . The troll comes in," the bear said in his most evocative storyteller voice, "and sits on the edge of the bed. He holds a coffee cup filled with warm water to her parched lips. He's whistling a tune and smiling, calling her his little darling, his baby girl. But the girl watches the zipper of his khaki pants. Inside his pants is a monster; the little girls in kindergarten told her that. Inside little boys' pants was a monster like a worm."

The air was a thick-petaled flower swarming with baby lizards crawling everywhere over the idiot grass: skinks and whiptails, chameleons twilling their minuscule dew flaps, hatching even now from a clutch of eggs. Just an inch long, they hunted insects, butterfly larvae and worms, baby crickets and katydids. They sounded like a trillion synchronized, reverberating rubber bands, but wetter and more mysterious. The troll spit a glob of marbled mucus into the weeds. The lumpy spit slid down a blade of fool's wheat. Dung beetles and mayflies hatched from tiny gummy eggs, caterpillars spun branches together to make gray mummies, and moths, convinced the porch light was the moon, beat themselves to death against the bulb. She couldn't think of what she was thinking; every few seconds she lost her way, her thoughts going on without her, being revealed behind a closed door, like when she waited outside her parents' bedroom while they whispered inside. It made her feel like she was already back with the earth. Earwigs crawled over her arms, gnats chewed her ankles, horseflies bit her neck. She was no different than this aluminum lawn chair, the frame tilting to a dangerous degree, no different than the deformed oranges, than the nightshade gone to seed by the side of the house.

The troll put his pen down and got up, walked over, and pulled the afghan up to her shoulders, covering up her chest. He wheezed. "Smoking," he said, rubbing his fat tongue over his rotten teeth. He moved one citronella candle, smelling of lemon and a needle's prick, closer to her feet, carried the second back to his table and set it down, careful not to spill wax on his work. In the flame she saw auras of tiny handwriting on onionskin paper. The letters were square and uniform. They looked more like a pattern than characters in the alphabet, and there was a picture of Michael Jackson torn out of a magazine and framed with carefully drawn roses and thunderbolts, a blurry newspaper oval of the president with 666 written on his forehead and one of the Virgin Mary surrounded by swastikas. At the top of the page he was working on was a Polaroid of her. He must have taken it while she was sleeping. Underneath, he'd written, GIRL.

The troll was anxious. He used a toothpick to weed out corn kernels from his teeth, smoked cigarettes one off the end of the other, and reeked of fearful sweat like garbage trucks in summer, like bad Chinese food and smelly feet. He drove leaning forward, headlights off, trying to navigate like a moth by moonlight. The passage was tight, branches flicked against both sides of the van, and the mud road made oozy sounds. The party, Sandy decided, was for the turtle because she was seventy-six. She wore false eyelashes made of spiders' legs and a wreath of violets around her head, and the caterpillar, who was so much younger and always looking for bits of wisdom to improve his rhetoric, asked what she'd learned in life so far.

"Not to eat bad grass," the turtle said.

They were sitting around the tree stump, drinking flat beer out of Styrofoam cups, and the bear, who'd found the precious liquid scattered among pieces of charred wood, seemed already a little drunk.

"Here, here," he lifted his cup, "I'll sing you a song. . . . *It was sad. It was sad. It was sad when the Titanic went down. Men and women lost their lives, even little babies died. It was sad when the Titanic went down.*"

"Why are you always so gloomy?" asked the caterpillar. "This is a birthday party, not a funeral."

The turtle looked depressed. Her husband had died not long ago and the funeral had been a fiasco.

"Cheer up," the bear said. "Today you're sixty-seven."

"Seventy-six," the caterpillar corrected him, "and remember what Lincoln said, 'If this is coffee, I'll have tea, if this is tea, I'll have coffee.'"

The bear and the turtle looked at him blankly. "Could you explicate?" the bear asked.

"Oh, you know Abe," the caterpillar said. "He was a nice man, though not always coherent."

But there was nothing to be done; the turtle was depressed, the big barroom bags under her eyes sagged, and she got teary. "Looks like rain," she said, glancing up at the sky.

"Yes," the caterpillar nodded, "everyone make sure to stay away from the swing set because it attracts lightning. If you touch a door handle and it's hot, never go into the hall; and if someone catches on fire, wrap them up quickly in a blanket. Don't go in the water if you hear thunder and try not to be at the top of any trees. Put out all campfires with water and don't throw your cigars into dry grass. Always watch out for stranger danger and be careful if you've had a big meal and feel light-headed and your blood turns into heavy cream. Don't take any pills the troll gives you."

The ones she'd taken earlier made it impossible to keep awake. Water moved against the shore in its white noise way and she heard a buzzing sound that at first she took for a fly inside the van, then a giant dragonfly hovering outside the passenger window, and then a speedboat towing water-skiers.

The back door swung open and bright light shone in her eyes. She felt her pupils quickly retract and she turned her head.

"You'll like her," the troll said. "She lies still." Water licked the wooden poles of the dock, where blue crabs fed on algae and barnacles, and nobody said anything. *They like me,* she thought, *because I lie still.*

And a new voice said, "That's Sandy Patrick."

"Down here nobody will know the difference," the troll said.

"What, are you crazy?" the man asked. "She's on the news once a week."

"You didn't take the other one either," the troll said bitterly.

"She was too old and he don't like them to have tattoos," the man said. And then the light was gone. The hue under her eyelids changed from orange to wavering black. She was four and had wet her bed again. *They like me because I lie still.* If the bed gets wet, throw the sheets on the floor, throw the afghan; then it will dry but the whole place will smell of urine. The man who owns this mattress puts water onto the bed. And it's horrible to sit all night in a wet diaper, but if you wet your underwear just try to go before bed. *They like me,* Sandy thought, *because I lie still.*

"Bad luck," the man said. He and the troll had walked around to the front of the van. "Call us if you got something we should know about."

The troll got in and slammed the door, turned on the engine, glanced at her in the rearview window.

"Never put your finger in an electrical socket," the caterpillar continued, "and look both ways before you cross the street. Don't swim on a full stomach because you might get a cramp and watch out for swaying weeds at the bottom of the lake, because sometimes tendrils catch your feet and pull you down. Wash your hands after you go to the bathroom and don't eat moldy bread. Never play with matches, hold sparklers at arm's length and scissor blades together and pointing down, and never run at the pool. Don't eat things you find in the medicine chest—it's not food, it's scientific—and always, always wear your seat belt."

"Home again, home again," the troll shouted with glee, "jiggidy-jiggidy-jiggidy-gee."

Seven: GINGER

All night long weather fronts battled for the soul of the house. The doorknob shuddered and wind tried to get at her, invading the glassy installation, snaking through vents in the paneling. Wet leaves, twigs, and tiny wood chips were strewn all over the backyard. A big branch hung off the walnut tree just outside her window, its pulpy-colored wood swarming with earwigs and centipedes. Underneath one of her mother's breasts, cancer broke through like bubbles of steak fat, so tender and oozy that they went through a box of cornstarch every day.

    When she was younger, she'd dreamed of Christ's body, the holes in his palms and between the tendons of his feet, but not only the gross parts, the sexy parts too, his flat stomach, even his cock. Nobody ever talked about that, the slight sheen of sweat on his red ball sac, the fine wrinkled skin in the crack of his ass. When you die your soul slips into a pitcher of water or the moisture inside a cat's eye; the soul waits until the body's buried or burned, then wanders the world looking for a human or animal who wants to have a baby. Sometimes the soul flies off to heaven, through the hospital window and up like a plastic grocery bag caught in a gust of wind. Or the soul goes with you right into the ground, becomes one with nature, growing up in every blade of grass and falling with every raindrop. The souls of the earth mingle and that's why nature tingles with intelligence, why ice covering a pond seems like more than frozen water.

The phone rang upstairs. The jangly cadence made her think of Mulhoffer's face, and she pulled the flannel flap of the sleeping bag up against her neck and puzzled a second until she remembered the trustees' meeting and how her father asked her to get there early, have coffee ready, and arrange some butter cookies on the silver platter. He figured waiting on the trustees graciously would soften their hearts and bring her back into favor. But she heard his car pull out of the driveway hours ago. A current of anxiety cut through her stomach. Once again, she totally fucked up.

Trucks whipped past, trailing ribbons of exhaust, splashing mud over the soft shoulder. She passed the mall; only a few dozen cars dotted the parking lot. The place had deterioated to several

empty storefronts and third-rate chains. It might go bust. The mayor
was already talking about turning it into a health club or a high school
annex.

Rainwater puddled in the drainage ditch outside the church,
and she had to straddle the muddy water to reach the latch on the
big aluminum mailbox. Just a catalogue for Sunday school supplies
and a flier advertising cheap group rates to Sweden. Tucking both
under her arm, she ran up the wet asphalt. It was littered with wind-
blown leaves and wet chrysanthemum petals, soggy gladiola, and
shriveled carnations that had blown out of the Dumpster.

Her father's car was gone, as were the trustees'. The meeting must have been long over and she guessed her father was making
up for yesterday and visiting the sick. There was a car parked near
the door, one she didn't recognize, and this made her apprehensive
about going into the church. A trustee might be waiting to ask if her
dad's car had air conditioning, if he drank wine around the house or
spent lots of money on new clothes. Once when she was little, play-
ing communion with her dolls on the altar, a trustee came into the
church and said she had no respect for Jesus. Inside, the butter-
colored Ford was meticulously clean. A small plastic garbage bag
hung from the radio dial and a shoe box of inspirational tapes by
Depak Chopra and Mary Anne Williamson were arranged alphabeti-
cally. It was probably Mrs. Mulhoffer's car; she came by often to
fiddle with the plastic altar covers, to settle everything in the sacristy to her touch.

Her father insisted on using as few lights as possible and never
turned on the heat until late November, so the narthex and stairs to
the basement were dark, still smelled of damp paint. He was into

self-denial, and not just at Lent, when he gave up his chocolate bars and secret cigarettes, but all the time. He ate canned soups and wheat rolls and on weekends wore ten-year-old khakis with threadbare black clerical shirts.

As she swung open the door at the bottom step, she saw Ted's mother waiting outside her office, reading the announcements tacked up on the bulletin board; Lutheran missionary work in Africa and pleas for support for the youth group car wash. When Ginger first took up with Ted, his mother was thrilled. A minister's daughter, a girl who'd have a cheerfully restraining effect on her son, who'd dress in shin-length floral dresses and quote Bible verses in times of trial. But once she'd realized Ginger rarely changed out of her jeans and sweatshirts, her tennis shoes and heavy-metal T-shirts, she'd told Ted, *There's something not right about that girl.*

Ginger, unlocked the office door, turned on the lamp, and motioned for Ted's mother to sit on the beige folding chair in front of the desk. The smell of burnt peroxide from a recent perm mingled with his mother's sweet perfume. She wore a denim dress with a nautical pocket seal and navy blue tennis shoes, with little white anchors on the toes. Like lots of women in the church, she dressed like a little girl, in smocked floral dresses and teddy bear T-shirts. She wore a red snowman vest on Christmas and a cotton bunny sweater at Easter. She wouldn't sit down, just stood there blinking, explaining that the store manager was threatening to press full charges. He said her son was a very sick young man.

"I just can't take this anymore," she said, taking a wadded tissue from her pocket. "First the drugs, then the police, and now that fellow Steve. All you have to do is look at him to know he's not right. All I ever wanted to do was help my boy, try and get him back on his feet. He's always making everything so hard for himself. There comes a point where people have to take responsibility for themselves. Ted doesn't seem to realize that."

"There's nothing wrong with Ted," Ginger said. "He's just miserable about his face."

His mother shook her head. She never spoke about the accident, always changed the subject to something more positive, like the kid on her block who got a track scholarship to college or the rich lawyer who took his mother for a trip around the world. "I just want him to be happy and healthy."

"Nobody's happy and healthy," Ginger said. "Everybody has problems."

"If you'd raised him you'd know his dark side. Things never work out for Ted. There's something off about him. It's not in my genes, but there were bad seeds in his father's family and I can't help thinking Ted has been blessed with some of that."

There was no arguing with her. She'd decided he was poisoned and had been working out the details of this theory for years. There was *something not quite right* about Ted and nothing would convince her otherwise. Ginger stood and moved toward the door. His mother followed her out of the office and down the corridor, lined by Sunday school partitions, full of long empty tables where hopeful little children made crosses out of Popsicle sticks and learned the words to "Away in the Manger."

"If you see him, tell him to call me, please!" Ted's mother said as they stood in the damp cement stairwell near the back door. Ginger nodded, but it was a lie.

She knew his mother had told Ted that his stepfather was his real father, and by the time he found out the truth, his real father was dead. His mother made him like he was, raised like a fallen prince, taught him to think he was better than everyone and so much worse. And she thought life owed her something too and was bitter because she'd been beautiful and cheerful but things never panned out. Ted wanted to save her but he couldn't, and she'd never forgive him for that. She was vain too, had lots of photographs of herself up on the walls, signed across the bottom like a movie star, and she was always talking about how she still wore the same size dress as when she graduated from high school. She played show tunes in the house, sang along outloud, and wouldn't talk to anybody during these recitals. If Ted tried to speak with her, she'd sing louder; her eyes turned the other way. Ted said that when he watched her now it seemed funny, but when he was little her singing scared him to death.

"So Mulhoffer was mad?" Ginger asked, as she stood in her father's office in front of his huge mahogany desk.

"Yes," he said, leaning back in his chair. "He believes if you dress like a moral man, then you'll act like one."

"Who died and made him God?" Ginger threw herself into one of the leather wingbacks, draped her legs over the arm.

Her father leaned back in his chair. "Mulhoffer went to the Wednesday night Deerpath Creek service and came back with raves. He says they make Christianity fun, like going to a Broadway show or a sporting event."

"What do you think?" Ginger asked.

"I've been out there. The head minister wore red suspenders and a blue striped shirt, like a Wall Street banker. They're using corporate philosophies to make everybody feel like they're moving up the church ladder, getting a raise or a promotion. But spiritual change is more subtle than that; you can't just check items off a list."

"Why'd you become a minister anyway?"

"For the free wine," her father smiled wearily, "and all those delicious tuna casseroles and Jell-O salads."

She laughed, but no matter how cavalier he acted, she knew he was worried, because the crease marks in his brow had grown deeper and that shell-shocked look never left his face.

"The problem is," he said, "is that Grace is impossible to explain."

"Are you mad at me?" Ginger asked.

Her father looked at her. "Not mad, just disappointed."

Ginger looked at the pile of theology books with felt markers stuffed between the pages on his desk. His Oxford English Bible was so old, the front adhered to the spine with black electrical tape. Packs of dove and lamb stickers for the Sunday school kids were scattered next to his mug of cold coffee. In front of him was a pile of yellow legal pads.

"Are those for Sunday?" She wanted to change the subject, knew he was always ready to talk enthusiastically about his next sermon.

He nodded, obviously pleased she'd asked. "I'm writing a parable about two girls. Want to hear a bit?"

Ginger nodded, watched him straighten his spine and begin

to read. This was his whole life now; his rumpled coat lay folded on the floor by a pillow and she knew he'd taken to sleeping near his desk.

The empty apartment smelled of stale beer and pot smoke. She put her palm against the rough stucco wall and moved down the hallway, past the outline of Steve's barbells. Lines of yellow light hallowed Ted's door. She turned the knob slowly, opened it a crack, half-expecting to see him on the bed, legs akimbo, blood and brain matter splattered up over the walls.

But the bed was empty, a spot of her own blood among the sheets soft-petaled flowers. One pillow was stripped of its case, leaving a rectangle of stained foam rubber. He'd taken tube socks and T-shirts, an extra pair of jeans and a couple of flannel shirts from a rag-snake that slithered out of the closet. The overturned shoe box spilled a pot leaf belt buckle, a Bic lighter, an old wallet. His ivory-handled hunting knife and the rubber-banded pack of get-well cards he'd gotten while he was in the hospital were both missing.

He was always talking about getting a cabin in Canada, a place with a woodstove and outdoor plumbing. He'd heard the hippie talk about all the eccentrics who lived up there, the Vietnam vets and the witchy-poo ladies who collected herbs and practiced white magic. Sometimes he wanted California, to sleep on Venice beach and work at one of the open-air bars along the strip. Since the accident he had a new plan almost every week; every scenario projected him out of his scarred body and into a place where his face was whole and beautiful and his every gesture imparted with subtle meaning.

Reaching down, she gathered the remaining items and put them in the shoe box, pulled the top sheet up over the blood stain, and turned off the little coiled desk lamp. She stood for a minute in the dark room, looking into the woods behind the condos. On the other side was the back of a fast-food restaurant, its green Dumpster and glittery blue-gray asphalt. Bright artificial light played in the leaves, and it was then, just as she'd turned her back to the window and was stepping into the hallway, that she heard someone crying, the voice like a string of tiny diamonds cut for a birthstone ring.

"Steve!" Ginger knocked on his bedroom door with the knuckle of her pointer finger. "Are you in there?" The sobbing stopped and the noises that followed formed an equation of panic, a tittery silence, a *shush,* then the bedsprings shifting against the floor and denim slapping up against skin. Steve walked across the carpet and opened the door just enough to frame his flushed chest. A blast of heat that reeked of come and blood wafted out, a scent she remembered from going down into a neighbor's furnace room, to see a cat give birth to kittens.

A line of blonde hairs ran down his stomach into his pants and his eyes were so bloodshot she knew he was both stoned and drunk. He tipped a can of beer up to his lips and smiled, glancing back toward the bed.

"What's so funny?" Ginger asked.

"Nothing," Steve said, looking down at the carpet and trying to contain his shit-eating grin.

"You got a girl in there?" Ginger asked.

Steve looked at her with a defiant smile and let the door swing open a few inches so Ginger could see the girl coiled under his army blanket, mascara smeared around her eyes and her face slick with tears. The inverted cross and pentacle plaque over her head, the black light poster of a wizard nearby, and that smell, dirty sheets, his blood-soaked hospital clothes, ribboned with the delicate scent of the girl's body like a single tulip dipped in salt water.

"I should go," the girl said, shifting in the bed to wrap the blanket around her as she stood, then turned away, bending over so her ribs pressed out of her back. She slipped her T-shirt over her shoulders and pulled up her jeans.

"You don't have to go just because this prude shows up," Steve said. "It's a free fucking country. Anybody can do anything they want."

The girl didn't answer, just finished dressing and slipped awkwardly past him and into the hallway. Steve's long hair hung in his face, obscuring all but his green eyes and shiny forehead, the hard curve of his upper lip. "The Minister's daughter," he taunted Ginger, "rescuing the lamb from slaughter. How touching." He laughed as the girl followed Ginger down the darkened hallway.

"You bitches can fuck each other in hell for all I care," Steve yelled.

The girl led the way through the darkest part of the forest, far from the condo lights and the backyard spots of the subdivision. Trash clumped in the weeds; rain ruined paperbacks and silver gum wrappers. These woods were domesticated; an old fort hung precariously in one tree, a tire swing in another. She chattered nervously, telling Ginger how on summer nights she'd snuck over to swim in the condo pool and play with the condo kids, who always had fire-crackers and porno magazines and could blow smoke rings. "Once we built a hut out of branches and wet newspapers and made Indian paste out of cornflakes and water. We did a lot of stuff," the girl said, "had wedding ceremonies and beauty contests where the winners wore necklaces made out of beer tabs."

The path led up into a backyard, past a picnic table and a swingless swing-set frame. There was no furniture in the split-level's rec room, no light on by the garage. The girl's jaw started to tremble and she said she didn't know what made her go over there. "Come and spend the night at my house," she begged. "Nobody's home."

"No, you go back," Ginger told her. "Make sure the front door is locked. You'll be okay." She touched the cool inside of the girl's wrist, the delicate tendons and subtle pulse. The girl swung into her chest, her damp lips in the angle of Ginger's neck.

The match's flame sent a prism of fractured light over the blackbirds' oily feathers. Orange sequined their wings as they huddled in their own shit on piles of bound newspaper. The deer's eyes like marbles dipped in mayonnaise, an earwig climbed up a nostril, and slivers of dried ligament were pasted with soured blood to the top of the TV. She felt in her pocket for the baptismal candle she'd taken from the junk drawer in the church kitchen. She'd thought she'd have to use the small Christmas Eve candles with the cardboard skirts her father kept in a box in his office closet, but the old baptismal candle was there in the drawer, meant for a baby girl with its tiny pink rosebuds and cream-colored dove. With a swivel of her wrist, she worked the candle into the red dirt, took the big tarnished serving spoon from her pocket, and stabbed it into the earth over and over until she could lever out wedges of dirt. With her fingers she picked out bits of broken glass, an earthworm, molten pebbles like tiny internal organs. Breathing through her mouth, she avoided the voluptuous stink of the deer and the blackbird droppings like scuzzy ocean foam. Dirt packed under her fingernails as she used the edge of the spoon to hack through a thick root. Chips of geometrical ice fluttered in the candle's light, first frost forming on the goat grass that grew along the inner barn walls. She coiled each half of the severed vine, like baby snakes, in the dirt. The blackbirds were upset, picked at their feathers, made subtle sounds like a lady in church searching for a hard candy at the bottom of her purse.

She placed the small plastic cross against the granules of dirt and pulled the flare out of the deer's head, ripped it off the top of the television. Its expression seemed to have changed; maybe it was a trick of light, but the stoic stare was tempered now by the mouth's smirky angle, the wry tip of the deer's head. There was a drapery panel of paisley material in a pile of rain-soaked clothes out in the dump, near the ash trees and the earth balls where she'd once seen a black snake, and she hoped to use the cloth as a burial shroud. Candlelight sparked the frosted sumac berries, the kudzu leaves. She walked out of the barn among skunk weed and fisted ferns, a baby's cracked car seat and water-wasted *Playboys*. The flame blew sideways and dimmed. She cupped her hand around the flame, felt the fire's heat in the soft part of her palm. She heard a sound in the trees and terror quivered through her. It wasn't the furtive moves of squirrels or the sneaky sound of rats gnawing into garbage, but the sting of electrified flesh, like a belly flop, or a slap across the face. The toe of her tennis shoe caught on a kudzu vine and as she went down, five warm fingers wrapped around her ankle. Leaves flew up as she flung her arms out and kicked with her free leg. A blackberry briar ripped across her cheek and a star zigzagged like white neon.

Eight: SANDY

With every thrust of his hips, soft pubic hair and balls hit Sandy's chin and she let out a gasp, her tongue a rag carpet, her chapped lips stretched into an O, the cracked corners stinging. Worms moved inside the earth, inching their fleshy bodies through the dark; they met and whispered like French lovers, twisting themselves into knots and bracelets. She kept her eyes closed, relaxing each part of her body like when the gym teacher played the wave tape and the girls learned yoga and stress management. Worms needed oxygen when their muddy tunnels slogged full of water, so on rainy days they sprawled out pink and obsequious onto the sidewalk, letting their ridged skin breathe. The rounded shadow of her umbrella fell over their pink bodies, and Sandy, in her yellow rain slicker with the ducks on the pocket and little yellow boots to match, crushed each under her plastic sole. Gray globulars glistening on the cement, usually a sliver kept its wits and squirmed for cover in the damp blades of green grass.

For fishing, you dug them up in the backyard, pulled them out of the earth and dropped them in a coffee tin with clumps of moist dirt. Her father showed her how to run the sharp metal up through the worm's body, so the whole hook wore a flesh-colored coat. If you got out of bed at night an Indian might grab your ankle and if no one left the night light on, then you'd stay in bed. Sometimes she dived headfirst under the covers, where there were colored fish like in the dentist's salt-water aquarium. *He likes me because I lie still.* Her brother put slugs in a jar, sprinkled salt on them, and watched as they blistered in the sun. He'd cut green tomato caterpillars with his Swiss army knife into tiny bite-sized pieces and helped their father pour gasoline on the Japanese caterpillars' webby homes in the backyard trees.

All morning the caterpillar bad-mouthed worms, how they lay around on the forest floor smelly and lazy as drunks. He felt superior because he had a hundred legs and a velvet coat of shiny blues and greens.

"But it's not nice," the bear said, "to be so uppity. What about 'all God's creatures great and small?'" They both leaned against a big maple, listening to rain slap at the highest leaves and watching the turtle open her stonelike mouth and press out her gray tongue to the beads of water that dangled off tendril ferns.

"It's easy for you to say." The caterpillar was always touchy about his genealogy. "You come from an old family, one known for its lack of common sense and lyrical appointments."

"I've never understood all that," the bear said yawning. "If we're all here now, aren't all our families the same age?"

"I admire your Socio-Marxist tendencies," the caterpillar said, stretching out on the collar of the bear's evening coat, as if he might nap. "But the most important thing to remember is not to take anybody else's toys."

"You make it sound so easy," he said sleepily, shifting his rump off a jagged rock and tipping his hat down over his eyes. "If only it were so." The bear sighed as if he were made out of caramel, a quivering baritone that intermingled with the prickly static moving in and out of the troll's lungs. Sandy opened her eyes. His belly rested on her forehead like a fat cow and she could see up the tunnel of his loose shirt to where chest hairs grew like ocean grass around his nipples. Each of his kneecaps pressed against an ear, magnifying the back-and-forth rub of his khaki pants. His hands gripped the headrest, pelvis repeatedly flattening down, then tipping up over her face.

The worm strained to multiply and even though she didn't really have breasts, she didn't want the little girl T-shirts anymore. She wanted a training bra and had snuck over to the lingerie department to look at them. Weary of the salesgirls and suddenly embarrassed, she fled to the toy department, the far counter where they kept the expensive baby dolls locked up behind glass. His pelvis cracked against her skull and the troll swung his knee over her face and knelt beside her, trying to catch his breath. She tipped her head sideways and gagged up warm Coke laced with come. The sky behind the windshield was a green-blue cellophane. He stood, hunched over, squeezed between the front seats, got his cigarettes from the glove compartment, his glasses from the storage shelf, and a beer from the cardboard twelve-pack on the floor. They didn't stay in motels anymore. He'd taken to sleeping beside her on the mattress, spreading the afghan over them both, curling up behind in a parody of marital bliss. He opened the driver side door and the harsh overhead bulb lit up the van, attracted a pair of tiny moths, made her feel like a girl in the water-stained porno magazines she found in the woods behind the house. He left the door ajar and walked out into the trees to smoke his cigarette, finish the warm beer, and pee inconsolably into the roots of a maple. Last night she'd seen the troll, sitting on a stump, wiping his eyes with one of his cloth handkerchiefs, shoulders heaving.

Turning her head away from the little puddle of puke, she saw the file folder where he kept his love letter. It must have fallen when he'd pressed himself between the seats. Her wrists were secured together with tape, but she managed to lift the folder into the ' ht and open it to the first page.

Michael Jackson told me he never liked Lisa Marie, but he had to marry her because the King came to him in a dream and demanded that he be her second husband. If he has on white, then it's the real King, the Love Me Tender King and you should listen to him. But if he has on green sequin trousers and a silk shirt then it's the fake king and you should disregard everything he says. You may wonder why I took the girl, that's very secret and only for the King to know himself, it may have to do with office poli-

tics in a certain giant corporation and that the board of
directors wants me dead. This is because I read the secret
documents and found out about my non-person status. I
challenged this 666 man to prove to me he had not tam-
pered with the weather map and I warned the world about
this Christ killer in 1978. People don't know, but Jesus once
had a girl he kept tied up. He did many things to her, like
sprinkle whiskey on her forehead and feed her plums. Even
though she was heavy he carried this girl on his back like
a baby and he'd test her to make sure she was real. The
Last Girl is a white cat with a pink tongue. Anyone can
fuck her anytime they want. The magazines are filled with
girls and no one seems to realize you can take one whenever you want.

The pages flew out of her grasp and there was the troll's face.
Orbiting bugs reflected in his glasses and a soft blue vein swelled above
his eyebrow. Why hadn't she heard the door open? The troll heaved
his weight up into the driver's seat. His jaw trembled and she smiled
to assure him it was all right. Already he turned his ring around so
the ruby was palm up and he swung his arm up over his head. She
closed her eyes; there were reasons. Before all this, whenever the
light fell a certain way across her bedspread, she'd think of herself as
a girl in a movie, watching rain beat against the window, the subdivision houses snaking off like a necklace into the horizon.

Sometimes she wrestled her brother down to the ground,
sat on his chest, and dangled a drop of spit over his face while he
twisted his head back and forth screaming for her to stop. She complained about unloading the dishwasher and taking out the garbage

and sometimes she said hateful things to her mother that hinted at the reasons Dad left her. A desperateness came over her, a feeling of knowing the limits of her own mind, and she'd say sneaky things to everybody aimed at making them feel bad about themselves. She lied too, told strangers that she lived on a farm, that her mother was a lawyer and her father away in New York City on business. She'd lost a lot of friends because she lied; they got suspicious of every-thing she said, then started avoiding her in the hallways at school.

This summer her mother kept asking her brother if he'd packed, if he had everything ready. She'd taken a bath, put on a new dress and red lipstick, then sat at the kitchen table flipping through a magazine, glancing up every few minutes at the clock. He'd come into Sandy's room and sat on the edge of the bed, told her how weird it was that Mom hated Dad, because he didn't even think about her that much. His relief at going home was so palpable it infiltrated ev-erything he said, made him flushed and talkative. He told about the video arcade in the mall and how they rented movies and watched them in the basement. Sandy felt pressure building up around her heart; she couldn't look at her brother and finally picked up the pic-ture he'd drawn her as a good-bye present, a depiction on tracing paper of two white horses drinking from a stream.

"Anybody can copy a horse out of a book," she said.

"You're probably right." He took the picture back and went into his room with the red truck wallpaper and Snoopy bedspread.

The troll cut the black electrical tape with his pocketknife, pressed a strip down over her mouth, climbed into the front seat, and started the engine. She told her brother the drawing was beau-tiful and tacked it up on her bulletin board between her Winnie the Pooh postcard and the one of leaping dolphins. Her brother took her hand and said you couldn't touch dolphins because they got head colds and sore throats from the germs on your fingers. Dolphins liked people and wanted to come up on the land and get married, eat cheeseburgers, sleep in warm beds. Her brother said their dad was getting sick of his new wife and soon they'd both be coming back home. The troll was talking too, as he backed the van. But Sandy only half-listened, lying as she was in the grass behind the mess hall at camp, reading the letter her mother sent from home. The bear was over in the raspberry bushes, complaining about the thorns, picking nubs in his striped silk vest, and eating all the biggest berries himself.

"The caterpillar," he said, "wasn't feeling very well. His symptoms are quite exotic: winged hallucinations and a longing for an Indian headdress. But to be honest," the bear said sheepishly, "I'm afraid I've stepped on him. This happened once with a rather congenial cricket. One misstep and the most satisfying friendships are gone forever. It makes you think about God," the bear said sadly. "It's so annoying leaving everything up to him."

Nine: GINGER

Ted spread his wool army blanket on the ground, picked up glass shards and sharp rocks, though he couldn't stop the razor-tipped leaves of the kudzu from snaking closer. Through the blanket she felt bent grass, stiff weeds, and underneath cold damp dirt. He slipped his hand under her shirt, pushed her bra up so the underwire dug into flesh above the nipple, coned and flattened her breasts so they felt like animal teats. Above them a blurry drunkard's star was framed by gray branches. Trapped between that heaven and this earth, they were like the sinful Adam and Eve, Ginger thought, but instead of being cast out, God confined them to the polluted garden, to these fouled and fucked-up woods.

"You scared the hell out of me," Ginger said as he undid her jeans, the metal button, the tingly silver teeth. This was a repentant fuck, so he treated her delicately and with great reverence like the common cup. Gently, he pulled her other tennis shoe off and pitched it into the kudzu near a rain-soaked sweater, then wriggled her pants down and crouched between her legs. By her head, a plastic grocery bag spilled out a roast bone, old spaghetti, yogurt cups, paper diapers that smelled of ammonia and melted butter. Junk mail and slimy plastic wrap were intertwined with the vines of kudzu.

Ted flattened his tongue and she felt his rough taste buds against her labia and looked down, watching how he moved his head like a dog drinks. And this thought was the raft that floated her over to pleasure. Sometimes it took a vision of herself, butt up, back arched, breasts hanging. Sometimes it was a rhythmic bar of his tongue strokes that pushed her out of this material world into the pure purgatory of sensation, that moment when the dirty words—clit, cock, and pussy—filled up with blood and became the language of desire. This reversal cast the fetid garbage, Ted's own palpable body odor, cigarette smoke, and sour milk into a metallic lick, the tangy taste of death's cock. The planet's gravitational spin swung her hand off the blanket into what felt like dry rice and wilted bok choy, ancient Chinese food in a splayed white paper carton. Ants ran from the scene, each holding a white kernel on their backs. Ted's voice box crackled like a jag of radio static. She put her hands into his long hair, cupped his scarred cheek against her lifeline, felt the stretched skin, the sinewy knots. Stray light from the condominium complex snagged in Ted's hair, his shirt fell open, exposing his bruised nipples; between them a crucifix, the minuscule body of a dying man nailed up on a tiny silver cross.

* * *

Steve sat in front of the fire in the barn, knees to his chest, shoulders straight, the position of Indian forefathers in museum dioramas. It was a small fire started with newspaper stoked with broken branches and an old tree stump. Flames encased them in red light and reflected in the snaggletoothed pieces of glass left along the edges of the TV screen. She could tell by Steve's swollen features that he was drunk and by his wide, dilated pupils that he'd recently snorted lots of cocaine. In front of him was a fairy circle of white plastic carnations and fallen feathers, in the center a carefully folded blood-soaked rag, the hospital's name stamped along the hem.

Ted's flushed face was weirdly translucent as he flipped the blanket up and spread it over the barn's dirt floor.

"Your dad was in the hospital today giving communion to some old lady." Steve squinted his eyes, as if trying to squeeze out tiny tear bullets that would pockmark Ginger's face. Ted grabbed her hand; it was a warning that Steve was in one of his crazy moods.

"What a bunch of shit." He poked the fire with a stick.

"Lay off her," Ted said. "She hurt her ankle."

"Fuck her ankle." Steve stood up, his spit hissing on the embers. "What about all that shit she said to you in the mall?" He pointed at her.

Ginger felt her face flare up, her heart pound against her ribs. *He's going to kill me,* she thought, *and Ted won't do a thing.*

In the backseat Ted arranged the army blanket and the peony pillows from his bed. Everything he owned was in the car and Ginger could tell by the fast-food wrappers on the floor and the half-filled plastic gallon of springwater that here's where he'd been hiding out. She got under the blanket and put her bad leg up on the armrest. Ted made the rounds, the long gray parking lots, the dark fast-food chains, and the strips of ratty woods, over and over until it was three in the morning. Ginger watched light play in the long strands of Ted's hair and Steve's body rising and falling as he slept, hunched against the passenger door up front. Strip-mall lights strung out mile after mile like a necklace of meteors. She felt trapped in a film loop, the scenery out the window painfully familiar, but for all the kinship she felt it might as well be outer space.

"I thought I heard someone trying to break in down here," her father said as he stood above her bed. "The door rattled and there was a knocking at the window and a voice like your mother's warning everybody to eat properly and not to bump the fontanel on the baby's head."

"You're dreaming," Ginger said, trying to see if he had on his striped pajamas or black suit. Slowly her eyes focused on his white clerical collar floating below his face like a leash. "Go back to bed."

"I can't sleep. Mulhoffer invited the assistant minister from Deerpath Creek to preach tomorrow. He said it would be a nice change of pace." Ginger heard the mellow sax notes of one of his jazz records in the stairwell and could smell that her father had been smoking cigarettes. "Promise you'll come," he said, stepping closer to her bed.

"You know I will, Dad," she leaned up on an elbow.

"Are you sure you didn't hear anything?" he asked. "Sometimes when I look out I think I see her over where she tried to grow those pear tomatoes, walking in and out of the tree line in her flannel nightgown."

Ginger's eyes adjusted and her father's face took form and definition. She saw that his eyes were closed and his chin tense and bunched.

"Do you think she was happy, Gin?"

"No," Ginger looked the other way, "she never was."

He cleared his throat and Ginger heard the mourning doves start up on the telephone wire outside, and the starlings in the maple and the ravens on the windowsill and the fat vulture that crouched on the streetlight waiting for another bloody roadkill. And her father said, "Go back to sleep. I'll just sit here for awhile at the foot of the bed."

The usher smiled, showed his capped teeth, and slipped her a bulletin printed with a close-up of a daisy. He nodded toward the altar. "Packed house." He winked. "Better duck into the cry room."

Inside the soundproof room a little boy with pale brown hair pushed a tiny cement truck around on the carpet, and in the front row a baby fretted—drool darkened its mother's shoulder. Ginger found a seat in the back corner below the speaker suspended high on the wall. A hymn sounded, its reception through the black cloth tinny and distorted like a transistor radio. Through the thick glass Ginger saw that every pew was packed, and even while the people sang, each head remained so still they might as well be stones with wigs attached. It was a German thing, complete physical command over even the most passionate scenario.

The Mulhoffers sat in their usual place up front, alluding subtle control. It was all passively situated in the slightly arrogant slant of Mrs. Mulhoffer's head, the squarely confrontational positioning of Mr. Mulhoffer's shoulders. Her father was only partially visible, an outstretched black shoe and a bit of linen cloth, one anxious eye and the bridge of his nose. This fragmentation gave Ginger the sense he'd come apart like a paper doll and had been hastily taped back together. Beside him the Deerpath Creek pastor, in a blue suit and red tie, exuded the low-key confidence of a corporate raider.

The organist pushed the pedals and the notes got thicker and the hymn rumbled to a stop. In the silence the cars on the highway could be heard rushing by, but the sound was subtle and unobtrusive as water moving in a riverbed. The man walked up to the pulpit and looked down into the first pews. Beside him on a small table were two boxes of breakfast cereal. He beamed at the audience, took his folded sermon from his inside jacket pocket, and bowed his head.

"Grace, mercy, and peace unto you from God our father, Lord and Savior, Jesus Christ. Amen." Her father visibly cringed, put both his hands to his brow, as if he had a headache. Today he wore his richest robes, the raw silk, the densely embroidered stole, and his heaviest bronze cross. But the material was wrinkled and it embarrassed Ginger that her father looked disheveled. It was like he'd come from the past and the trip through time had soiled his apparel and wrung his body out.

"People are strange, aren't they?" the man began cheerfully. "We tend to judge a person by their outward presentation. In other words, we'll size them up by the type of car they drive, the clothing they wear, even the brand of cereal they eat. Think about it, if a fellow drives up in a sixty-thousand-dollar Mercedes 480XL, gets out wearing a Nautica button-down sports shirt with designer polo pants and a matching belt with Timberline on the heel of his one-hundred-fifty-dollar loafers, the guy is too cool, he's the cluck of the roast, the talk of the town, he's on the fast track to the top.

"But if you were to take the same exact fellow, have him drive up in a rusted-out 1979 Pinto with a K-mart sports shirt, Sears on the rump of his bell-bottom blue jeans, Made in the USA on the rubber heel of his ten-dollar tennis shoes, he's a graduate of Cotton Belt Tech and Beauty School and eats a generic brand of cereal. The guy's a bona fide nerd, a geek with a capital G. None of the girls would want to go out with him, no one would want to associate with him, we would call such a person a loser. But it's the same guy in different wrappings, so what's in a name?

"*It appears everything.*

"We have here a generic box of cereal, Crisp Rice." He held the box up for everyone to see. "Now you would think with the savings that are offered with generic goods that they would take the food market by storm, but the reality is that generic food only makes up three percent of U.S. food sales. We're kind of suspicious of this stuff, aren't we? Maybe it's substandard? Let's get honest; there's no telling where they got it. Maybe they put the good stuff in the brand-name boxes and swept the generic stuff off the floor. We don't know this product. We're suspicious of it. We don't trust it. So we *don't buy it.*

"Same is true of the generic God. A few years ago I saw an interview with a famous movie star just before he died of cancer. When asked if he believed in God he answered, 'Why yes I do. I believe someone is in charge of all this, he and or she or whatever rules over all things, I do believe there is a God.' People all over the country were thinking at least he believes in God, at least he's going to heaven. But my dear friends, there's nothing further from the truth. People today are being deceived by this generic God. By saying *I believe in God* and thinking they are on their way to heaven, and that is an *Absolute Lie.*

"You've seen those commercials on television where some famous athlete gives an endorsement for a product. Now can you imagine if I did a commercial like that? 'Hi, my name is Joe Shmoe, running back for the Virginia Vanguards. What do I eat before I go out on the field before the big game? I eat this.'" The man held the black-and-white box up and turned as if to speak with some-one off-camera. "'What is this stuff? Does it have a name? No name? Oh.'" Then back to the congregation. "'I eat this cereal. It is cereal. And cereal's gotta be good for you so go out and buy some today.'

"Now would that make you go out and buy this product? Obviously I didn't even know anything about this product—it wasn't a part of me.

"The same holds true for a generic God. Ninety-seven percent of all Americans, according to a Gallup poll, say they believe in God. The Bible tells us God wrote into the heart of every person that he exists. Everybody knows there is a God. You see evidence of it all over the world. You can go into the darkest corner of the Amazon, where no man has ever gone, and you'll see something that represents God: a totem pole or a sacred rock. Climb the Himalayas, you'll see people falling down in front of a bronze, hand-crafted object, giving tribute to God. Everybody knows there's a God. The problem is not everyone knows the *Real God*. They know everything about God but they don't *Know God*. How about you, my friends? Do you know the real *brand-name* God? I know you sense his presence *but do you know him*? There is a heaven- and-earth difference, my dear friends, between having knowledge of God and *knowing God*. And the consequences are exactly opposite.

"You know, earlier I tried to do a commercial for this generic cereal and failed. Why? Because I didn't know what it tasted like or anything about it. But if I were to do a commercial for this one"—he held up a box of Kellogg's Rice Krispies—"I grew up with this stuff. I've heard commercials about this ever since I was a little boy. I eat this stuff, not very often anymore, but I used to as a kid. Now, if I were to do a commercial on this, I think I could come across more convincing. And I'd be more prone to buy this cereal, because I know the product. It's a part of me." The man bowed his head.

"Let us *brand God's name* into our hearts. God grant this for Jesus' sake. May the peace of God that passes all understanding keep your hearts and minds in faith in Christ and Jesus. Let us stand before the altar and profess our faith. I believe in the living God, creator of all human kind, that creates the universe by power and love. I believe in Jesus Christ. . . ."

Mrs. Mulhoffer turned to look at her husband and Ginger saw that her cheek was flushed, her eyes bright with enthusiasm. Mr. Mulhoffer nodded slightly to affirm her, but he disapproved of such shows of emotion and he straightened his shoulders and sat up taller against the pew. Tiny hairs stood up on the necks of all the middle-management men. And in the cry room their wives gazed dreamily at the Deerpath Creek pastor walking in long victorious strides back to his seat. He looked like the sensitive guy on their afternoon soap and he'd spoken their language, TV commercials, cereal, sports. The word *pandering* came to Ginger's mind.

Her father's eyes were closed, his shoulders hunched forward as if he were trying to protect himself from the words of the sermon. The organist started up with an unfamiliar tune, more like a pop song than a brooding Germanic ballad. The guest pastor smiled to himself and her father, turned his body, and glanced out the window at the blurry cars speeding away on the highway, her father's face set in a superior expression that even Ginger sometimes hated, the one he wore when he tried to explain that TV was bad for you, that reading was better than video games, and that Disneyland was purely for pagans.

Ten: SANDY

The hunchbacked troll staggered in wearing a paisley shirt and a brown suede vest, smelling of crabgrass and wet fur. Nervously, he jiggled the cat's-eye marbles in his pocket as he leaned against the back wall and rooted around in the stack of dirty magazines. From a brown paper bag he pulled a tiny orange and peeled it with great reverence, lifting every last stringy ligament off the fruit. He offered her a wedge, pressed it between her chapped lips; his fingertips tasted of salt and smoke, and the orange so much like *happiness* that she started to cry. Anything could set her off now, birds tittering behind the boarded window or the sound of water rushing through the pipes in the wall. He stood over her and said he hated to see her so sad and would she like to hear his silly song, the one to the tune of "Twinkle Twinkle." She nodded her head and the troll began to sing.

Swim Swim Sad little fish / How I hoped to make a wish.
That this girl will spit up gold / Into a dish or into a bowl.
Swim Swim Sad little fish / How I hoped to make a wish.

He used an outstretched pointer finger to conduct himself and giggled so hard afterward that his lips spread up and his weedy teeth showed. From the bottom of the bag, he pulled a pomegranate, broke the red leather skin, gobbled up a handful of crimson jewels, and spit the seeds into the carpet. He offered her a few of the bloody kernels, but she shook her head and lifted the afghan up to her nose; static like crazed punctuation flew out of the blanket's wool weave.

She'd shown her brother how to make sparks between the blanket and the sheet, told him she was a witch, that she could do other tricks, make a tiger appear on the living-room couch or a dolphin leap out of the bathtub. She could fly out the window if she wanted, all the way to China. One day, when their mother was gone, she promised to show him how to levitate his cereal bowl, how to get a ghost to make his bed.

The bear claimed to be a warlock. If you had a headache, you could call him and he'd put a clove of garlic into a silver bowl of olive oil and say a prayer to Saint Teresa of the Little Flowers. He didn't want any payment, only a little respect, and he did this for her daily because she always had a headache and a sore throat and a runny nose. But the bear wouldn't listen, just shook his head and explained about the pink room upstairs where lavender clouds moved lazily along, and the unicorn waited, watching over the little girl who French kissed her pillow every single night. There, he said, a thousand butterflies sang a song about angels and rosebud bedspreads as they swayed in unison over a rippling lake, and a white pony with a pink mane and eyelashes long and black as a movie star's drank, and the blue unicorn, its horn made of crystal, ran through the shallows, sending up sprays that sparkled like diamonds.

"Your old dad is going to teach you about the birds and the bees," the troll said, tapping his forefinger against her knuckles, trying to get her to hold his fingers like a baby, his mouth fixed into a stiff smile, as if he'd only seen the facial expressions of people on TV. "Hey dolly. Hey cutie pie," he said as he stroked the skin of her cheek, told her she smelled like butter, that her skin drove him insane. Tears glazed his gray eyes and he looked up into the ceiling and whispered, "Little baby girl."

In his new manifestation as a butterfly, the caterpillar was only interested in sentimental stories of transformation, tales that made his mascara run and turned his tiny nose pink. "When Donna Polito gave birth to her second child," the butterfly began, his blue and silver wings making a glittery and glamorous backdrop, "she felt a singular moment of joy at baby Miranda's first cry and then nothing. Her world went black and she slipped into a coma. Infection ravaged her body. She needed a machine to breathe. After fifteen operations, the doctor told her husband to make plans for her wake. But he couldn't do it. 'Maybe love will succeed,' he thought, 'where medicine has failed.'" The butterfly looked at her with the pleading eyes of a TV evangelist. "So that night he recorded the voices of his two young sons and the next day brought the tape to the hospital room where his wife lay near death. '*Mommy come home!*' they pleaded on the tape. Suddenly his wife's eyes fluttered open." The butterfly paused to dramatize this moment by batting his own long lashes obsessively. "You see, she'd dreamed she heard her children's voices and she looked into the eyes of her husband and whispered, 'Take me home.'" The butterfly dabbed at the corner of his eye with a wisp of fluffy milkweed and said, "Something similar could happen to you, but only if you hope hard enough, my dear." And he flew out of the pink spotlight and the unicorn stepped inside the circle of light and nudged his wet nose against her cheek. His crystal horn sent out rainbow slivers like a prism.

"You were chosen, for your similarities to raindrops and day-old kittens, to the first white crocus and a baby's tender heart," the unicorn began. A gold filling in his mouth shone like a piece of glass in the sand. He raised his creamy blue hoof and balanced it on the edge of her mattress. "These are the qualities of a princess," the unicorn confided, "and so we directed the troll to you."

The troll fed her pear slices and a few cubes of Swiss cheese from a cracked floral plate. He wore the clip-on bow tie, the red shirt with the lima bean–shaped grease spot, and sat on the edge of the bed, gingerly, as if he didn't want her pee stains to soil his clothing. As always she was mesmerized by the reflection in his glasses, today the image only vaguely familiar. The wet gag hung around her neck as she shredded the rubbery cheese and limpid pear flesh against her back teeth. She leaned forward slightly and asked him what had happened to the cat. His eyes startled and he yanked his head back as if a chair had talked or a piece of pizza. Setting the last pear slice back onto the plate, he lifted the cloth from her neck and retied it tightly around her mouth, the corners pulling like a horse's bit. He stood, walked to the boarded window, his hands in his pocket worrying the marbles.

"I'll let you go if you tell them you ran away from camp and spent all these weeks counting dead leaves on the forest floor and making friends with little animals," the troll began thoughtfully as if he'd been practicing this speech all night. "If you can tell me the name of the bird with the highest IQ, or the exact weight of the one-legged Indian chief's beautiful daughter," he stared at the inside of her wrist where the tendons stood up like piano strings. "I'm going to let you go," he said in a firm voice, meant to convince himself, "but not until the very last minute."

"No talking allowed," the unicorn said, because to fly he had to meditate, think about angel food cake and milkweed spores, of loosened balloons and grocery bags caught in the wind. The mall from above resembled sand dunes, and the myriad condominium complexes, patches of mushrooms. Wind stung her ears and jerked her hair back. She crouched behind the unicorn's head, her hands fisted in the long hair of his mane. His fur smelled like old snow and was sooty and damp, pricked up on end with effort. Below the cloud cover, school buses lined up behind the cement-block building and a smudge of gray became the flapping American flag. She was surprised how shabby and ephemeral all the buildings looked, like an overturned junk drawer filled with gray ribbon and ugly dime-store beads. There was the 7-Eleven where she and her brother played pinball, drank Slurpees, and ate silver-wrapped Hershey kisses. She recognized her block by the strange triangular cul-de-sac, and the unicorn spiraled down until he hovered like a dragonfly just above the split-level's bay window. Inside, her mother slept on the couch under her winter coat, her face above the navy wool so slack and lined that she looked like a different person. On the coffee table was a drawing Sandy made in kindergarten of a stick figure with arms coming out of its gourd-shaped head and a naked doll with stiff black hair. Watching her mother's hand clutching the coat's material to her chin, Sandy realized that for a long time before she'd gone to camp she'd felt sorry for her mother. In her head she created a string of pink hearts and red rose petals, and clasped this necklace around her poor mother's neck. Through the doorway, Sandy saw her little brother sitting at the kitchen table eating a TV dinner. He'd turned his head to look at the poppy-colored refrigerator, a fancy one with double doors and a tinkling ice machine. There, held up with a magnet, was a pencil drawing he'd done of her face and at the bottom he'd written *Sandy Come Home*.

The troll carried a blue plastic bucket and sang "Rock-A-Bye-Baby" as he entered the dark room. He bent over and turned on the pink shell night-light. Steam rose in fragmentary tendrils from the pail's lip. He sat on the edge of the bed and sank the yellow dishrag into the bucket and crushed a stream of water out with his fists. He washed her hip and thigh in tiny round strokes as if he were buffing a beloved sports car or stripping an antique table. Through the cage of her lashes she watched his face flush and his eyes fill up with tears and she felt grateful and wanted to tell him it was all okay, that God could still forgive him if he'd change his ways at once.

"That's exactly right," the butterfly, who was always looking for any opportunity to proselytize, interjected. "Miracles happen every day! Take the little baby who crawled onto the open window ledge, tried to reach out and touch a bird on a nearby branch and began to fall.

"'No, baby!' a man screamed out and ran forward. He arrived just in time to catch the infant in his cradled arms." The butterfly sighed dramtically, "Now isn't that a sweet story?"

Sandy nodded her head and the moon sent a ring of light into the room that moved across the floor like a rock's ripple on water, and she tried to get the dream back but the unicorn had lost his concentration. Crippled with exhaustion, he needed to be led through the dark wood.

Eleven: GINGER

In the dream she was singing off a printed sheet at the new-age center. The melodies were like campfire songs and the lyrics full of eagles soaring above mountaintops and lines about beautiful souls dancing in celestial moonlight. Cheerful men in pastel sweaters took her father away to the county hospital. She felt the lyrics bite into her scalp, slither into her brain like baby snakes. As the group chanted their affirmation, she managed to sneak out of the cinder-block building. But all around the perimeter stood a chain-link fence. Spirals of barbwire laced the top, and on the other side a Doberman with a bloodied, bandaged foot foamed at the mouth and stuck his snout angrily through the metal mesh.

Throwing off the sleeping bag, she limped up the stairs, still wearing the thrift-store blouse with the Peter Pan collar and her mother's floral skirt, the waistband twisted to one side. The house reeked of phantom pot roast and ink off the *Sunday Times*. She hallucinated tinkling silverware and her mother's lilac perfume. Turning on the faucet in the kitchen, Ginger washed out her father's coffee cup and scrubbed the oat bits stuck to the edge of his cereal bowl, then let water gather into a glass and carried it to the rec room, where she sat under the gloomy Easter lily painting and contemplated putting on one of her father's jazz records. She liked the blue duo-tone covers and the way the scratchy music crackled out of the speakers. Sipping the chlorine-spiked water, a light froth spun on the cloudy surface; she noticed that the latch on the window behind the TV was open. Hairs on her arms pricked; her flesh goose-pimpled as she walked over and slammed the frame shut, twisted the metal lock. Anyone could shimmy up the drainpipe, latch onto the deck rail, and slip inside the window; that's how a convict escaped from a chain gang had raped a lady the next state over. He climbed onto the deck, opened the sliding glass door, found a steak knife in the kitchen, and accosted her on the bed, where she was folding clothes still warm from the dryer. The lock on the kitchen doorknob lay horizontal. Her father forgot to lock it when he went to church. Ginger slid the button vertical, which stiffened the flimsy latch bolt, not that somebody couldn't kick the hollow plywood door down or break a pane and shift the lock. The dining-room window was locked, but at ground level one smash of a hammer and a stranger would be standing beside the table with the white lace dolly and the bowl of plastic fruit.

Ginger saw this same sort of split-level built at the end of the subdivision. Each house took two weeks: first the pine skeleton, and then they stapled up the pressed-board walls and stuffed them with pink insulation. Using a chain saw anybody could cut through the house's exterior. As a child she set garlic on the window ledge to repel vampires and kept a baton under her pillow to bash intruders in the head. She practiced fire drills incessantly. Her father tried to calm her by insisting God watched over her, but Ginger knew if she had to believe in God and the angels, then devils and monsters existed too. Besides, God was always letting all kinds of bad things happen. It would be different if car crashes and murders were written off to chance, but what scared Ginger as a child was that God just sat on his golden throne and watched these things happen. Sure, *he watched over you* but that didn't keep *you* safe. Actually it was even scarier to think of somebody staring at you all the time, like the disapproving ladies in church.

Ginger walked down the hallway to her mother's bedroom. Her father kept the window cracked open to air out the room, trying to rid the space of mothballs and that medicinal ointment, but Ginger saw it as a way to lure her mother's soul back, give her a chance to hover around the bedspread ruffle or be absorbed into the wood grain of the dresser. Ginger lay down in the position her mother took in the last days of her life, slumped sideways, one leg hanging over the edge. She imagined her blood growing sluggish, her own heart stopping, veins fraying, and her soul lifting up with the slippery pluck of an avocado pit out of the greasy green pulp. But what if her consciousness gave out with her corporeal envelope? What if her mother'd become a piece of meat like the hunks of steak wrapped in cellophane at the grocery store? On her last day, Ginger rubbed her mother's feet with peppermint oil and brought flowers from the yard, lilacs and sweet-smelling hyacinths. She brought items that

might stir her memory, photographs, the little ceramic deer that sat
on the mantle, her beloved blue glass beads. But no object could link
her mother with this material world; only Ginger's hand entwined
in hers allowed her mother to close her eyes and breathe with a little
less effort.

The window in her father's bedroom was locked; he'd even
wedged a branch into the side groove to assure that if a pane broke
the window couldn't be raised, he who assured people that there was
an afterlife, that faith in Jesus could set you free from life's worry
and fear. His bed was unmade and she knew he hadn't been back to
the house.

After the service, Mulhoffer, surrounded by trustees, listened to the Deerpath Creek pastor talk about how his congregation
used marketing techniques, phoning local residents to decide what
services the church would offer, how their business components were
thriving, the health club, the day-care center, the mechanic's shop,
all of which attracted more people to the Lord. She'd slipped past
them and into her dad's office, where he was standing by the window with a cigarette, blowing smoke through the screen, his body
as languid as the smoke.

"I am utterly demoralized," he said. "They don't have to
fire me because if I ever have to share the altar again with that jack-
ass, I'll quit." He couldn't handle competition. Ginger knew that
was why her father had chosen the ministry, because it kept him
above the fray of the free market. And too, he preferred dealing
with women and children; other men always made him nervous.
Exhausted, he was probably napping on his office floor now, dreaming of the Latin mass or Bonhoeffer's plot to assassinate Hitler.

Up close, the sodden branch spilled wood pulp, and his bed reeked a little. Ginger knew he hadn't changed his sheets in weeks. She worried that like Christ, her father would allow brutish and ignorant people to hurt him or that he'd take martyrdom to the extreme and harm himself. He'd seen enough suicides: fat Mr. Reinholt electrified by a clock radio in his own tub, and the German lady who'd used her son's BB gun to shoot herself in the corner of the eye. Just this summer a teenager hung himself with an electrical cord off a beam in his basement. There was something contagious about suicide, like those kids who gassed themselves in Bergen. Her father's faith might not sustain him against the congregation's endless onslaught of private misery. He'd even admitted that sometimes he felt like a human trash receptacle and that he knew his flock was roaming away.

A lady in pink sweatpants on her way home from aerobics at the health club picked Ginger up along the highway. Her car smelled like cream as it just begins to curdle, and the woman talked about her word-processing job at the insurance company and how her husband, a guy named Chuck, had recently found the Lord.

I didn't know he was lost, Ginger thought as the lady pulled up in front of the welfare hotel downtown.

"This is no place for a girl like you," the lady said. Ginger assured her she was meeting her father at his church down the block and that it wasn't dangerous down here.

"No more than the mall parking lot where that woman got molested," she said.

The lady looked skeptical but unlocked the doors and let Ginger off at the curb.

Staring up at the brick hotel filled with dim blue light as if the moon lingered inside, she saw that only one window on the second floor was illuminated by a dangling bulb. A man in a wrinkled white shirt and dark dress pants stood by the window. Like her father in his robes and the old Germans from the church downtown, the man looked antiquated and exhausted by his connection to history, so different than the pastel suburban types sprung fully formed out of the mall's water fountains. Ginger figured something catastrophic had happened to the man, something that ended his life's narrative, that trapped him in a time out of time, somewhere around 1958.

Next to the hotel was the wig shop run by a Chinese man who smoked opium and did tattooing on the side. Before the accident Ted saved for a little red dragon with sapphire blue eyes. Styrofoam heads with starchy, flamboyant wigs peopled the storefront window. Usually there were several men who stood outside the liquor store, but because of blue laws the place was closed until Monday morning. A red-faced guy in a windbreaker sat in an old Pontiac parked out front and flashed Ginger a cynical smile that set off his hacking smoker's cough.

She felt like she was walking on a movie set, that the buildings were one-dimensional. It was that creeping Disneyland feeling again, where everything was make-believe, one attraction as false and inauthentic as the next.

In the parking lot, adjacent to the liquor store and across from the church, lay a dead pigeon and a bunch of rusty engine parts.

A fire blazed up out of a chemical canister and two round-shouldered men in hooded sweatshirts passed a quart of beer between them. A couple of naked dolls hung in the bushes under the boarded-up windows of the church; hair cropped with blunt children's scissors, their fat bellies streaked with mud. Below the arch of headless angels, the red doors were padlocked and so she walked around to the side door, where graffiti tags spread over the gray stone. Ginger swung the side door open, saw the light on in the hallway and her father's black raincoat thrown over the radiator. She glanced into his old office, where an open box of bulletins and an ancient carbon copier lay in the middle of the floor. She climbed the stairs to the choir loft, narrow and smelling like oiled wood. The angle of the curve always reminded her of the spiral stairs to fairy tale towers. Somebody lived up here. A blanket was folded over a pew and a paper plate of chicken bones balanced on the organ keyboard. Ginger tiptoed to the railing and looked over at her father standing alone in the light of a single candle.

The silver cross was gone, as were the tall candleholders and the red glass eternal flame. The slab of marble that served as the altar table and the cherry-wood carvings of the apostles had been ripped out. Everything was sold to pay the new church's mortgage. Her father spread his black shirt out so the dark sleeves hung over the raw wood. He stood in his white T-shirt. The tiny glass decanter of red wine and the tin of communion wafers sat ceremoniously on the black fabric. His lips moved silently as he held up a round wafer, broke it, and offered half to the wall. Ginger tipped back on her heels to see that he'd taped up Sandy's school picture and was now pretending to make her eat. Eventually he placed the wafer in his own mouth and picked up the silver chalice, offering it first to God and then to Sandy's lips. Ginger sunk her fingernails into the fat of her palm as she watched him drink from the cup, then place it carefully back with the other implements, shiny and strange in the candlelight, as the innards of a freshly killed cat.

As she came around the side of the church Ginger lost her footing on the weed-ridden sidewalk. In the lot across the street she saw Sandy Patrick hovering between two men, her blurry figure flittering among orange flames. Pale and insubstantial as an angel, Sandy wore her mother's oversized raincoat and a pair of electric blue pumps. Foundation streaked down her neck, silver eye shadow glittered under her brow, and on each cheek was a heavy spot of sparkling rouge. One of the men laughed, the girl said something, and Ginger recognized her voice from the hippie's house and from Steve's apartment.

"What are you doing here?" Ginger asked the girl, who looked less surprised than sullen, obviously trying to decide whether to acknowledge Ginger or not.

"Trying to score some weed," the girl said.

The man with the blond mustache and ratty eyes shook his head. "Oh man, we don't know nothing about that."

"These guys said they'd give me stuff to smoke." The girl looked at Ginger, sucking on a strand of her dirty brown hair.

"You're hearing things, girl," the second man said, his pale, pockmarked face squeezed like toothpaste out of his hood.

"You said you were going to give me some weed," the girl raised her voice.

"Now you just calm down," the first man said.

"I won't," the girl said and started to scream. Both men turned and ran along the parking lot fence and disappeared into an alley. The guy waiting outside the liquor store started his engine and drove off.

"Shut up!" Ginger said, trying to grab her arm, but the girl swung away and slipped her fingers through the chain-link fence.

"I'm staying here as long as it takes," the girl yelled, "and you can't do anything about it." She swung her hair and kicked her leg out awkwardly. "Fuck you." The girl screamed so loud the noise shot up like a bottle rocket, sent vibrations through the dark air.

"Let's go home." Ginger pried the girl's hands loose from the metal mesh.

"No! I don't want to go home," she said. "You go home."

"Come on," Ginger said, her tone implying that the girl was childish, "you're acting stupid."

The girl quieted down, but she wouldn't come off the fence, just hung limply, staring into the fire. Ginger stood with her hand on the girl's narrow wrist and watched her father walk furtively out of the church in his long black raincoat, his Bible with the electrical-tape spine and the leather communion kit under his arm. Ginger realized he didn't believe his prayers worked in the new church on the highway, that to satisfy himself and his God, he had to come down here.

"Okay," the girl finally said, "just don't tell my mother. She gets mad if she thinks she has to worry too much."

* * *

Bugs tangled in the yellow halogen streetlight and Ginger watched a man stagger out of a bar to pee against a parked car. His shirt was opened to his belt, his face so pale it seemed like he wore greasepaint and a little black eyeliner. Midway down the old highway, after the car dealerships but before the strip malls, the road degenerated for half a mile into Quonset-hut bars and shops that rented porno videos. The girl talked steadily about how her mother's boyfriend was a dentist, that he wore loafers and smelled of the grape fluoride he used to pack patients' teeth. Ginger gripped the girl's wrist and pulled her across the deserted highway. She just kept talking about how even though her mother's boyfriend's hair was receding, he still pulled the fringe back in a gross little pony tail and that he thought he was so intelligent just because he'd seen every movie in the classic section of the video store and always won when they played Trivial Pursuit. Worst of all was how her mother wanted to sleep over at his fancy condo almost every night and when she was home she acted like a goofy teenager, giving herself facials and asking if her new jumpsuit looked sexy on her.

"It's just gross," the girl said emphatically as she steadied herself against Ginger's shoulder and slipped off her mother's backless high heels.

They continued walking along the soft shoulder and she got quiet for a while, then started asking Ginger questions about Ted. How long had he had the scar and why had he shot himself in the face? Ginger said it'd been nearly a year now and that she wasn't sure why he did it, probably just to see what it felt like. The girl said wasn't love a funny thing, horrible and wonderful all at once, like her parents—they'd made the cutest couple but they had to break up because they never agreed on anything. Ginger looked down and saw that the girl's toes trapped in the nylon panty hose looked like the delicate hoofs of a deer. She told Ginger about the boy she liked from school, how he was teaching his dog hand signals and that by using the computers at school he could activate the fire alarms any time he wanted. He stole CDs for her at the mall. The only bad thing was that she'd noticed particles of wax suspended in his ears. Once they made out at a boy/girl party, but she still wasn't sure if he liked her because they didn't really have a choice—everybody paired up on the couch or chairs or laid out over the rug.

Ginger half listened. They were nearly home now and the fast-food restaurants were coming up, each set on its rectangle of striped asphalt, bold signs advertising Coke and burger combinations, happy kid meals, two-for-one fries. Ginger thought she saw a cat jump up on the Dumpster in back of Burger King. But the animal couldn't be a cat; it had coarse, furred hind quarters and thick nailed hoofs.

"What's the matter?" the girl asked.

"Let's just keep going," Ginger said.

The mall came into sight, lit up like a blank movie screen, the loading doors glimmering in weird green light. The girl sensed Ginger's apprehension and, in cockeyed solidarity, told about a creep in her neighborhood. "Once, a long time ago," she started, "a girl was selling candy for her school and she rang his doorbell. He answered the door with his penis hanging out."

"Let's just be quiet for awhile," Ginger snapped. "Can we do that?"

Twelve: SANDY

As the principal made his morning announcements, castigating the students about the home-economics teacher's stolen purse and the rampant food fights in the cafeteria, the unicorn snuck by the school secretary and slipped into his office. Rainbows emanated from the crystal horn, so potent in color that they intoxicated the fat principal, made him drop his donut mid-sentence and fall forward onto his page of notes.

"I have some sad news to tell you all." The unicorn took the antiquated microphone from the principal's clenched fist. "Carl Levitt shot himself while cleaning his gun yesterday afternoon and Sally

Dyers died last night of the leukemia that has kept her bedridden for so many months. It may seem cruel," the unicorn said, "but eventually everyone has to make the transition from animal to mineral."

The troll nodded emphatically. He wore a black beret today, cat fur stuck to the wool. He sat on the edge of the mattress holding her hand and said, "There used to be a real nice girl who stayed in this room named Sandy Patrick." His glasses reflected a patch of her dirty T-shirt and a slender white arm. She braced herself by arching her back and cataloging her brother's features and the way her furniture was arranged in her bedroom, but these were loose footholds on a slippery slope. Memories wore dangerously thin; like a notebook left out in the rain, letters ran together, geometry proofs smudged, only an occasional configuration reminding her of the freckles on her mother's collarbone or the time her class went to the flower show and she'd watched a tiny Japanese lady in a red silk jacket arrange orchids in a way her teacher called sublime.

The troll said "like a big girl" she could eat with him at the kitchen table tonight. He was making Mediterranean spaghetti with black olives and capers and she smelled the onions turning translucent like chips of ice, the garlic moving around the house like a bully. The food activated a sideshow in her stomach. The fat lady laughed deeply and the flame swallower, a Latin-looking man with a singed mustache and a red silk shirt, gave her a knowing look. The girl in the silver leotard balanced on the high bar, swinging gracefully this way and that.

In a spirit of festivity he left the door to her room open so she could listen to him cooking and the TV tuned to QVC. A retired lady called and said the teddy bear she bought looked so cute on her bedspread and how, since her hip replacement, QVC kept her company day and night. Sandy smelled the browning sausages and heard the troll sing one of his stupid songs. *One little sausage sizzling in a pan. Sizzle. Sizzle. Sizzle. Sizzle. Sizzle. Sizzle. Bam!*

She imagined herself swimming up from the bottom of the pot, careful to avoid chunks of garlic and bits of basil leaf, climbing up on a sausage log, wringing olive oil from her hair and lying out in the warm range light. The butterfly brushed his powdery wings against her cheek in a showy if insincere butterfly kiss. His hands were folded and his eyes wet.

"Fifteen-year-old Jennifer Rodkey of San Antonio, Texas, waved to her father, then jumped into her boyfriend's pickup truck," the butterfly began, ignoring her sour facial expression. Like the bear before her, she wanted to let the butterfly know to keep it short. "As the twosome headed to school, danger was the furthest thing from their minds. But as her boyfriend rounded a steep curve, the truck gained a will of its own and skidded off the road. The truck flipped, trapping her beneath its crushing weight. *This is it, I'm going to die,* Jennifer thought in terror as her eyes got blurry and she passed out. Her boyfriend, John, crawled from the wreckage, but Jennifer was not breathing and had no pulse. *She can't die, not here, not now,* he thought to himself. He gripped the edge of the roof and lifted the one-ton truck off the ground. A second later Jennifer drew breath and cried out. 'Everything's okay now, sweetie,' John said, holding the truck up until the emergency crew pulled her out."

The butterfly closed his wings dramatically and bowed his tiny head. "Can I tell you one more?" he asked, rushing into his own moment of silence. "About the lady in New York City who survived a subway collision, or my best one about the teenaged drug dealer who planted a dahlia bed in an abandoned, trash-filled lot." Before Sandy could dissuade him, the troll's footsteps frightened the butterfly and sent him flapping into the dark corner where the bear, the unicorn, and her little brother all waited, opaque as ghosts and just as helpful.

Mattress springs shifted, crunched, and the troll knelt next to her, all the time whispering his strange prayer. GodhelpmeforIhavesinnedandIdonotknowthedifferencebetweenwaterandwineandIamanonpersontryingtoberealGodhelpme. . . . The bat flapped its wings fiercely against the cave wall, the rat just behind him, rapacious and noisy in the garbage. The troll choked monosyllables from his clenched throat, using his black magic to go back, turning himself into a sea lamprey, a mollusk, a carnivorous plant that loved flesh and bled curdled cream.

It was long after midnight before she found herself staring at the candlelight wavering over the carefully set kitchen table. The troll poured a little more wine into her teacup as she examined her plate of spaghetti, saw the black olives and tiny green capers, but there were also what looked like cat's-eye marbles, limp crickets, and furry spiders' legs floating like junk in the tomato sauce.

"The girl that used to be here was an ugly duckling," the troll said, "afraid of everything, always worried." He waved his hand, "But she's long gone now."

Sandy flayed tendrils of consciousness around her mother's favorite dress, sunset pink silk with a scalloped neckline, and the citrus scent of her father's shaving cream. When these didn't work, she dug her fingernails into the skin of her forearm, but even pain was ineffective in connecting her former life to this one.

The troll wore a velvet bow tie, his eyes magnified by his glasses, teeth like bits of charred wood. He stared at her and asked why she wasn't eating.

"I'm not hungry," she said, looking at what must be a mouse's pink tail curled in with the spaghetti noodles.

"That's absurd," he said. "You haven't eaten in two weeks."

"My stomach has shrunk to the size of a kidney bean."

He smiled. "No matter, soon all this will be yours," the troll said, motioning to the sink full of dishes, his love letter spread out over the Formica.

QVC sold plastic taco stands and queen-size cabana sets. His anxious attention exhausted her and she wanted to go back to her bed.

"It's perfectly natural for a girl to watch her figure," he said, covering her free hand with his own long-fingernailed one and using the other to lift her chin up. Unshored eyes and the swaying candle's flame reflected in his lenses and she smiled at him as convincingly as she could.

Thirteen: GINGER

"Looks like creepy man has a date," the girl whispered as they squatted on the cement front porch and peered into the big bay window. All the houses were dark except the dandelion of muted light in the window of this split-level. Ginger watched the old man, dressed like Klass in bow tie and plaid vest, pour beer from a beaded can of Budweiser into a teacup. A white candle dripped liquid wax over a green wine bottle. The man was talking animatedly, tipping his chin down as if listening intently, then throwing his head back and laughing. Though she couldn't see the sides of the table, Ginger knew this was a lonely heart's dinner, or like the tea parties she'd had as a child, arranging dolls in chairs, setting a table of tiny ceramic cups and saucers and making polite, one-sided conversation about the weather and the price of limes.

Though the man was clearly disturbed and there was no excuse for leaving your penis out *ever*, Ginger felt sympathy for the old guy. The way he dressed reminded her of her father's vestments, old-fashioned and slightly seedy, and she realized that the new church members connected her father's antiquated robes to something gothic and dangerous. Ginger's minister's-daughter mechanism churned, turning the man's perverted past into pity. He'd never been loved enough.

"What do you think he's saying?" Ginger whispered.

"Something creepy," the girl hissed back, "impressing his date with his knowledge of pornography or his love of small animals." At first thrilled to see the old man so dissolute, the girl's grudge no longer gave her pleasure and she was getting bored, glancing up the block at her own dark house.

"Let's goooo!" she said loudly. And almost simultaneously they heard a thud, saw that the man had bolted up so fast that his chair fell back behind him. His face quivered, underlit by the candle's flame. The girl screamed and ran across the front yard. Without moving his eyes from the window, Ginger watched the man extend a long-fingernailed hand and extinguish the flame between thumb and forefinger. Ginger turned toward the street but hesitated.

"Come on," the girl screamed from where she'd paused at the end of the driveway. "Are you crazy?"

Ginger heard the man's footsteps crossing the living room and she bolted up the driveway and joined the girl by the mailbox.

They ran full speed over the sparkly asphalt. The girl, young enough to still enjoy being chased, shook her hair out and laughed as they beat back driveways. The road tilted up toward the moon, hanging like a gypsy's earring among pinpricks of light. Blood beat against her temple and the intense effort of her legs made Ginger feel light-headed, as if her body flew weightless down the block. She felt more guilt than fear, remembering the night she'd gone with Ted and Steve to the state-subsidized condo complex. Steve made her ring the first doorbell; then they'd all hid behind the boxwood bushes. A middle-aged man came out, bald head surrounded with black fringe wearing a pair of nylon pants and a white dress shirt. His face was grayish, his eyelids so sunken Ginger figured he hadn't slept in days. "Who's there?" the man asked, flaying his open hand out as if to test the temperature of the air, and Ginger realized he was blind.

The girl led her across the yellow grass, up the front steps, where gasping and giddy she pulled a rabbit's-foot key chain out of her raincoat pocket and fumbled with the lock. Ginger glanced back. The man hadn't left his house, though she saw his silhouette behind the curtains, one keen eye in the material's slit watching as the front door swung wide and they rushed inside the house.

"Would you care for a ride?" Mulhoffer offered through the window of his paused Cadillac. "Lucky for you I was late at the factory."

Ginger hung back by the guardrail. After checking all the window locks and helping the girl wedge a broom handle in the track of the basement sliding glass doors, she was making her way home along the highway.

"I enjoy walking," Ginger said, "but thanks anyway."

"It's one o'clock in the morning," Mulhoffer said, annoyed. "Get in."

Ginger looked across the road at the deserted mall parking lot; there was no way around it. She pulled open the heavy car door and slid onto Mulhoffer's deluxe leather upholstery, sat so close to the window she felt the cold air coming off the glass. Mulhoffer smelled of wood chips and industrial-strength glue, a stack of his company's furniture catalogues beside him. A cross hung down from the Cadillac rearview mirror, and he had rolls of quarters piled in the spotless ashtray.

"How are you?" he asked formally as he accelerated up the highway. They passed under the streetlight into darkness and then back again into the light.

"Fine." Ginger glanced at Mulhoffer. His jaw clicked and he cleared his throat. She felt herself trembling. As a little girl she'd put books inside her underwear before getting spanked, and in the same spirit now she tried to build up an exoskeleton that would make anything Mulhoffer said easier to take.

He obviously disapproved of her roaming the highway. He disapproved of her low-life boyfriend and her lack of respectable girl-friends. As a minister's daughter she was expected to act like a *lady*. Even her father was less concerned with the authenticity of her reli-gious sentiment than with the appearance of propriety. And though her father made less than a shoe salesman, much effort was spent in grooming her with Latin and ballet lessons. She was encouraged to socialize with doctors' daughters and to date lawyers' sons. Her father read chapters of Jane Austen to her before bed and her mother's highest compliment was that Ginger looked like a member of that horsey set. She had grown up with the presumption that the circumstances of need under which the family existed were inappropriate to its quality. She had been taught by her mother to look forward to some betterment of this condition. But her mother's long illness changed all that, cracked and splintered the varnish her parents worked so hard to apply, and Ginger realized she had to give up her phony friends, her intellectual pretensions, and trade her white gloves for bread.

"You know," Mulhoffer said, "I don't think you're a bad kid. In fact, I think you're a pretty serious gal and that you've probably taken the words of Jesus a little too seriously." He used the same gentle and instructive tone he employed when flirting with his secretary. "You know that if Jesus came down today he wouldn't say the same sort of things he said back then. No," he slowly shook his head, "Jesus wouldn't want us to give away all our possessions, that's impractical. If Jesus came down today he'd be a big fan of technology. Heck, I think he'd enjoy a little TV. Let's face it, life is usually a pretty raw deal and good entertainment is as close to heaven as most people are going to get here on earth." Mulhoffer put the car on cruise control and sank back into his sheepskin-covered seat.

"That's why I manufacture the most comfortable chairs and sofas in the world. I don't care that they look like dead elephants. As long as when a man comes home, he can plop down in my chair and flip on the old Technicolor dream machine."

Ginger snorted.

"You don't watch much television, I take it," Mulhoffer said ruefully.

"No," Ginger said, "I can't stand it much."

"That's too bad," Mulhoffer said, shaking his head. "I've noticed at the factory the fellows who don't enjoy a little TV are always the ones making trouble."

Ginger smiled.

"You think it's funny?" Mulhoffer asked, his voice veined with anger. "Your attitude, young lady, is disturbing. As a representative of the Lord you should have more dignity. You need to shepherd those around you to higher standards. Christianity is evolving. Times are changing. These days people want entertainment. The new members still have mud on their shoes and they've brought their creek-bank mentality with them. They may have gone to college, but they've just come to town and they want to see the same thing they always came to town to see—a good show."

"So what are you trying to say?"

"That we don't need your father explicating theological passages or exploring his own mystical connection to evil. His sermons are off base. Religion has more to do with personal well-being now. That's why telemarketing is so important to our cause. We need to find out what our community needs. Aerobics classes for the ladies, basketball leagues for the men. We need to lure people to us by offering them services, like baby-sitting and marriage counseling. It's like the visiting pastor said to me after the service last week: Faith is a forward-moving phenomenon. It challenges us to press the very edges of innovation."

"How do you expect to bankroll all this?"

"That's where TV comes in. We need a half-hour spot on the local channel to telecast our service. Let your father invite the TV viewers to come out and visit us Sunday mornings."

"Let me out," Ginger pointed at the McDonald's, "I need a milk shake."

"Sure," Mulhoffer said, clearly pleased with himself. "I'll take you through the drive-thru."

"No thanks," Ginger said coldly. "I want to get out."

Mulhoffer snarled at her angrily, his white knuckles clenching the steering wheel. "Let me tell you, young lady, that I won't sit back and watch your father run the church into the ground. Mrs. Mulhoffer wants me to move with caution. She's always had a soft spot for people like your father. She calls them *antiquated* and *dear*."

"Right here is fine," Ginger said, focusing inside the restaurant at the sleepy couples in back booths drinking giant-sized Cokes and sharing piles of ketchup-strewn fries.

"I just hope you'll pass all this along to your dad," Mulhoffer said as she grunted and slammed the door. She felt his eyes between her shoulder blades as she knelt in front of the restaurant's glass doors, let her breath fall into a melody with her heart and began to pray. Mulhoffer kept his hand on the horn so long the sound made her light-headed and she thought she might faint.

Behind McDonald's, just inside the tree line Ginger came upon a configuration of objects. In the middle was a dead cardinal, a muted female, its belly split to expose shiny red innards, gluey and crimson as menstrual blood. Nightshade berries circled in the soft dirt followed by a wreath of white plastic roses. In the roots of a maple tree a motor-oil can filled with pee balanced in front of a ravaged doll's head. Someone had scribbled swastikas into her forehead with green magic marker.

Fear spread like sun rays out of her nervous heart, infiltrating every vein and capillary. She felt a dreamy reverence because the Protestant ritual of wine and water was wearing out. The dead bird's nightmarish holiness demanded silence. She bowed her head and touched her cold fingertips to her lips.

Steve clenched barbells in his fists and with a fast, synchronized flex of his elbows swung them to his shoulders, then back down to his thighs. Wearing a pair of cut-off sweatpants, the fabric hung low around his sculptured waist. His flushed chest held a sweat sheen and the hairs were so blond they lost definition and reflected like neon light. He must have worked late at the hospital and couldn't sleep. The night shift was particularly bloody: car crash victims, shootings, stabbings—all these happened almost exclusively at night. And the sight of blood leaking from flesh, spilling off the tin tables and dripping ink-spot patterns onto the white floor, was always miraculous to him. He usually came home invigorated, ready to pump weights for hours.

Ginger watched him stare at the TV. His biceps stiffened up like dinner rolls. His face reminded her of the wolves she'd seen on TV. He took pride in his physical perfection. Transparent enough to project your desires onto, he made you feel part of a glamorous world, usually available only through the spy hole of television. His girlfriends behaved like actresses, exaggerated their gestures, and spoke only in flippant one-liners that were supposed to sound like movie talk. And in a town like this, where everyone felt like the party was happening somewhere else, Steve was a lethal character.

"You're the last person I expected to see here." Surprise registered in his eyes.

"I thought you might have heard from Ted," Ginger said.

Steve shook his head. "He don't want to hear from you."

"Can you just tell me if you've seen him or not?"

"He split town."

"Without telling me?"

"Yeah, well, he met up with a sweet little piece of poon-tang at the mall." Ginger could tell Steve was lying by the way he looked over the top of her head at the cars parked outside. "He got himself a girl that won't preach at him all the time."

"Is that right?"

Steve nodded. "I'm available though," he said, pushing his hips forward, puffing up his chest, "if you're interested in a dance with the devil." He reached up and grazed Ginger's neck with his hot fingertips, but she recoiled and ran over the grass, back into the woods.

The clouds outside darkened the altar. During prayer she heard a truck fade into the distance. Her father stood in the pulpit in his rumpled linen robes, unshaven, goggles of gray around his wet eyes. He was trying to convince the congregation that their minor missteps allowed evil to flourish.

"We give evil a name," her father said with a tinge of real desperation in his voice. "Evil always comes at us directly." He wiped his brow. "Lucifer searches for a chink in the armor!" Ginger saw a trustee shake his head in the direction of another.

"As modern people and as children of the Enlightenment, we are not as realistic about the power of evil. We figure that if we ignore evil, especially our personal brand of it, it will simply disappear, or at least lie low. We blindfold ourselves from it. In fact, the more it's hidden, the more vicious it becomes and the harder it looks for a whipping boy."

She'd heard every kind of sermon. Her father preached on obscure theological points and horrific current events, the bombing in Oklahoma, the massacre in Luby's, now Sandy Patrick. And while his subject varied, his theme never did—the familiar form of evil and how everyone is implicit in the lie.

"We deny the evil lurking within us because if the truth were to be exposed, we would be consumed and obliterated from this community. We would be swallowed by evil itself." His pause was supposed to signal a tone change, but when he looked up he saw indifference stiffening the people's faces and, like a lounge singer desperate to hold a crowd's attention, he raised and animated his voice. "But the truth is that we can live together in such a way that the world's deep structures of evil begin to wither away. We do it by being faithful to each other. We do it by casting off power and intimidation. We do it by surrendering our claim to any kind of superiority over anyone. We give up our desires to make excuses for our behavior and we give up our constant claim of innocence, a claim we make despite the sure evidence that we are up to no good. In other words, we decide to be accountable to each other—all of us. We can do these things and more, because in Jesus, God has given us the grace to do them."

Resistance hung in the air like humidity. The congregation pushed their backs into the pews and braced themselves as if the church was an airplane hijacked by a religious militant. The tips of Mulhoffer's ears were red as bell peppers; he was furious her father hadn't taken his advice and preached about future growth, or at least copped the mega-church pastors' down-home style and talked about television or sports. Even Mrs. Mulhoffer, who always hid her emotions behind a smile, looked surly.

Her father quickly intoned the benediction, then hurried down the pulpit steps to the bench by the altar. He hid his face behind the hymnal as the organ started up.

> *Thou most kind and gentle death / Waiting to hush our latest breath /*
> *O Praise him, Alleluha / Though leadest home the child of God /*
> *And Christ our Lord the way hath trod /*
> *Praise, Praise the father, praise the son /*
> *Praise the spirit, three in one.*

The people sang off key, unable to disguise their hostility. She'd asked her father when he planned to move on to another theme and he said, *When they hear this one.*

Fourteen: SANDY

The troll threw a banana onto the yellowed newspapers. Sandy crawled over, frantically peeled down the fragrant skin, and shoved the fruit into her mouth, almost choking. The troll laughed, *my little monkey girl.*

Chained by the ankle to an exposed pipe in the basement, Sandy squatted on the cement floor next to the bucket filled with pee. She sucked the moisture from inside the banana peel and watched to see if he held anything else in his hands. She was the little monkey that sat on the wheelchair of the man with no legs in front of the gumball machine at the Walmart. The monkey wouldn't sit on the man's shoulder, wouldn't take the peanut from the man's lips. She jumped from the Pez machine to the top of the tall one that sold Pepsi and Diet Coke.

"Good night princess," the troll said, closing the door. The light went out and she was alone in the dark basement. How could she make the smelly stuff in the bucket into milk and where could she find a horse made out of white chocolate and a pink teddy bear that could sing the national anthem without looking at his notes?

She curled up on the newspapers. In a dream she spit gold coins and dried rosebuds fell out of her ears. She smelled like lake water, like a girl who'd been swimming all day in a pond where cows drink and frogs splay out from lily pads. Bits of leaves and blades of grass stuck to her cool skin under her bathing suit. Every word she whispered was trapped in a bubble and the bubbles formed a long necklace and her hair unfurled and she heard his footsteps above her, pacing this way and that.

Everything was right here. Furry blue elephants hovered like kites above her face, moving to the bouncing melody of "My Funny Valentine." She turned her head, watched Elena the ballerina twirl as the notes grew farther apart and more sluggish. Inside her jewelry box, along with the gumball machine rings and the silver cross her aunt sent from Illinois, was the pink plastic bracelet she'd worn in the hospital, her name written in black magic marker with the officious slant of a nurse's handwriting.

"Stop," she said, "if you're going to be like that." The sound of her own voice, muffled and discordant, was like the mumbling of the retards in special ed who walked as if their legs were attached upside down. The banana warmed her, snaked through her body.

The floor didn't seem so cold and who cared about the white spiders hanging upside down from the water pipes and the mouse in the corner that sometimes ran over to gnaw threads off the afghan. Her brother said, "Just lie still." And the darkness came into her like a mop's wet tentacles. The white kittens shouldn't be hard to find, or the baby-blue chick. And what about the little chipmunk in the floral apron who made tiny pink cakes, each layer no bigger than a quarter? It was cold down here and she let her teeth chatter like the Halloween sound-effects record her father'd bought the year they turned their living room into a haunted house. Sandy Patrick rubbed her arms and then her calves. But there was no way to warm herself; better to go sit in the lawn chair in the backyard, let sweat dampen the crotch of her bikini, let the deer look at her with his big brown bedroom eyes.

Inside the Barbie suitcase with the fat metal zipper lay a bathing suit with sand in the crotch, a pair of Snoopy shorts, and a T-shirt with a jelly stain. Underneath was her blanky, the silky top of a blanket worn to threads.

If you fell asleep too early at the slumber party, then the mean girls stole your training bra and put it in the refrigerator. They put plates of onion dip beside your cheek so when you turned your head, cool sour cream stuck to your eyelashes and oozed up your nose.

The boy was there, the one who sent the letter that read, "I luv U because your eyes are brown as the sequoias, your lips the fiery red of hell, and yourself like I like them best." In the closet, during her seven minutes in heaven, he gave her an Indian handshake and made jokes about slobbery kisses.

As the night wore on the girls got crazy, dancing to their favorite songs like lunatics, arms flying everywhere and legs akimbo. They screamed out the lyrics and Robin told a story about how her mother bled through her white Easter pants suit, how their dog tried to get the used sanitary napkin out of the trash. The girls' faces twisted up with exhaustion and they started telling each other that they were stuck up. Robin got so overheated that she went completely nuts and tried to strangle Sandy with a jump rope and the basement door opened and the troll came downstairs, holding a candle that illuminated his hunchback and runny eye. He scooped her up, carried her over his shoulder, walking in a slight incline deeper into the basement and farther into the woods. Her cheekbone bumped rhythmically against the small of his back as she listened to starlings call one to another. Leaves trembled and the troll squashed tender green seedlings with his heavy boots. She held the afghan to her face and sucked her thumb. Snakes hung like moss off tree branches.

The troll hurried along the path littered with plastic potato chip bags and french fry wrappers, then stopped abruptly. She heard his key chain rattle as he unlocked the little wooden door. The troll set her down in the dark and lit a paraffin lamp and she saw in its glow that the walls and floor were made of red dirt, the bed of green moss, and in the middle, before her, a giant tree stump for a table and fat logs for stools. On the table oatmeal waited in a little wooden bowl, and the troll pulled the silver spoon with the filigree handle out of his shirt pocket and handed it to her, then sat down to watch her eat.

* * *

"I got a letter from him," the bear said sadly. "It seems we've grown apart." He was smoking rose petals in his acorn pipe, puffing on the bamboo reed. From his birch-bark poach, with the leaf-stem latch, he took a pinch of yellow petals, struck a wood match against the tree stump table, and leaned forward to light up. The smoke smelled like sunshine heating up one's hair, and of yellow finches with singed feathers. "Letters from the other side," he said, "are always filled with gobbledy gook."

All afternoon the bear catalogued his sorrows. Summer was long over, so there were no more berries, just bark and weedy plants to eat. He was horribly lonely and missed the caterpillar so desperately, some nights he barely slept a wink. But she could tell by the preoccupied cast of his eyes and how he held his snout straight out that the bear loathed himself for sinking down so deeply into self-pity, and he said in a voice meant to chide himself, "For goodness sake, let's not whine about it. I have my health and my reputation. Life goes on. The earth circles the sun, the planets go around. It's all like some complicated game with different colored balls played by invisible and benevolent giants." He puffed a huge cloud of creamy smoke. "Maybe that's why I feel so anxious all the time."

Sandy offered some herbal brew in the chipped teapot the bear brought as a housewarming present. He found it wrapped in a moth-eaten cashmere sweater inside a bag of trash. But he waved her off and took the well-worn envelope from his pocket and began to read. "I have my memories. You dominate them. The space you fill in my mind is overwhelming and now being alone is the best way for me. I can live this way. But I still pull you out from my memories to spend time with you. The best times. The happiest times.

When you and I were all that mattered. I miss you today, today especially. I want to hear your voice and listen to your words. I want to see your face and touch your cheek. There is a park here with a tree for you to sit lazily under. I would watch as you stray from the directness of the sun." The bear's voice cracked and he trailed off but tried to act indifferent by rolling his eyes and flipping his wrist dismissively. "That sort of sentimental gibberish always puts me to sleep," he said, faking a yawn. "If he really cared, he'd come back for a visit."

Little Miss Nobody, the troll kept saying, his hand tight on her upper arm. First she heard the whoosh of the match, then a lush crinkling of paper and the smell of smoke. The red ant bit between her shoulder blades. The sting was accompanied by a smell like hair singed in a curling iron. Her brain went sliding backward, dissolving into vaporlike heat off summer asphalt. A spark snapped out of the fire and bit her knee and her father pulled her back, said that campfires were dangerous, that once he saw a little girl who wasn't careful get fire in her hair.

Over her shoulder, she saw the red bee floating toward her back and felt its sting a second time, the pain a star shape, hot and cold, and then the troll cleared a rag of phlegm from his throat and the cigarette tip illuminated his fingers and he pushed the fire into the valley between his hairy knuckles and a pinched growl came out of his throat.

Save me Jesus. Save me Lord. She smiled at the spiders dangling like acrobats above her head, listened to the mouse's minuscule feet gallop against the far wall. The bear wore a velvet top hat and his emerald ring. He said reading the letter put him in the mood to recite a little poem he'd composed all by himself. *Never eat porridge from an ivory spoon. Don't drink all the sumac wine or you'll die too soon. Kneel down by the tiger lilies on hot summer days. Don't ever bother reading those boring Shakespeare plays.*

Sandy heard the troll lock the basement door. She blew her own warm breath down between her breasts in an effort to heat up her heart. A teaspoon of light glinted on the shovel lying against the far wall. She was a little monkey. She was a little bird.

Fifteen: GINGER

Mulhoffer, using an unsharpened yellow pencil to point out figures on a flowchart, spoke enthusiastically about the church's future. He had a folksy delivery and low-key self-confidence that was undeniably contagious. His bald, egg-shaped head flushed pink with enthusiasm and every once in awhile he hitched up his pants. This gesture gave his presentation a sort of agrarian earnestness that worked like an aphrodisiac on the crowd. Men and women sat on pew's edge nodding at the architectural rendering of the future church complex. Designed by the same person who built the mall, it was a nondescript cement-block behemoth with long thin windows and an indoor water fountain.

Darcey Steinke

She sat in the back pew near old Klass. Taking a taxi all the way here from his garden apartment downtown had exhausted him and he dozed silently; a spot of drool grew on the lapel of his dandruff-flecked jacket. Her father sat in the front pew and, as usual, played it all wrong. His features set in an arrogant mask, he gazed out the window as if Mulhoffer's speech was of no interest to him.

But Ginger knew better. His flushed neck and trembling chin implied that he was nearly hysterical with worry.

In the pew ahead sat the couple with adopted children. They were *nice;* the woman brought over a tuna fish casserole when her mother died. The woman's husband, thinking she needed direction, cornered her in the church parking lot and spoke animatedly about his marketing firm. But Ginger could never follow his words: tele-marketing, annual quotas, targeted merchandising. The words evaporated as he said them and she'd just stare at him blankly and nod her head. But he meant well, they all did. There wasn't a single person present who didn't smile at her on Sunday mornings. So why did she feel like they were all zombies waiting in line to suck her blood?

At the end, just after Mulhoffer proposed buying TV time on the local channel and hiring a small, three-piece band, he praised her father for his devoted service to Good Shepherd. Mulhoffer winked at the congregation as he joked about her father's intelligence, his love of reading. "I can't even pronounce the names of the guys he studies, let alone get through a page of their books." Her father, Mulhoffer said, had done a fine job at Good Shepherd, had an obvious love for God's word, but he was clearly overworked and needed a helpmate, a CO-pastor.

* * *

The teakettle rang out on the little hot plate her father set up on the edge of his desk, next to the Lutheran seal paperweight and a pile of church-supply catalogues. He turned off the heat and poured water into his mug, stirred the instant coffee crystals until each one dissolved, added a packet of creamer. Now that they were alone in the office, waiting for the congregation to vote, the wind dropped out of her father, left him exhausted and spaced out. A blanket from home lay folded neatly next to the desk and he brought a pillow from his bed. She realized, watching him pick through his mail, that he'd been sleeping here not because of his obsession with God's word and its connection to the salvation of Sandy Patrick, but because he thought that if he kept vigil he could somehow heal the rift between himself and his church.

Her mother always claimed that her father was singularly unsuited for the ministry. Because he was so sensitive, so easily able to cry, sad situations made him act stiff and officious, which alienated him from the very people he was meant to comfort. Most ministers, worn out by the perpetual worries of others, created a cheerful persona and spoke in coded clichés about God's will, but her father was still uncomfortable with his position as God's representative, thought it slightly embarrassing and somewhat absurd.

Ginger swung her legs over the edge of the wingback chair and her father glanced up at her as if he'd forgotten she was there.

"You know I'll have to quit," he said.

Ginger nodded. But what would he do? At the end her mother had laughed in his face, said he was unfit not just for the ministry but for every other job too. He was a dreamer. "The world," she'd said, "has no room for men who believe in angels."

"But it's not the end of the world," her father said, trying to sound parental and reassuring. Maybe it was in the pestiferous nature of the ministry, maybe the lack of imperatives in the spiritual life, but even as a little girl, he never made her feel safe.

There was a knock on the door and he said, "That'll be Mulhoffer. You should go."

"Let me stay with you, Dad," she said. Fear and dread nibbled at her heels. She was always terrified of his vulnerability and wanted now to protect him any way she could.

"No," he shook his head, "you—"

The door opened and Klass hobbled inside. "Excuse me, Pastor."

"It's okay, Klass. It's just my daughter. Please come in."

"It's a shame, Pastor," he said, leaning heavily on his cane, his face filled with nostalgia, "it's enough to drive me over to the Catholics."

"Oh, Klass," her father said, laughing, "anything but that."

Ginger didn't feel like going home and reading over the employment ads in the newspaper, as her father suggested. She wanted to check on the girl who'd called last night and read her horoscope and an article from her mother's fashion magazine about spring sandals and the importance of proper accessories. There was an edge of terror in her voice when Ginger said she needed to get some sleep. She asked a flurry of questions: Did she believe in love at first sight? Were rich people happier than poor? If God existed, why would he let planes fall out of the sky and cars crash on the highway? Why would he allow people to get married who weren't really in love? When Ginger insisted she had to get off the phone, the girl said she heard a noise, something rattling the window, somebody creeping around in the basement.

Ginger rang the doorbell. "I'm giving myself a beauty treatment," the girl said as she opened the door, mud dried chalky on her cheeks, wetter around the ridges of her nose. The girl's eyes were as bright as green crocus knobs pushing up under a cover of dead leaves. She explained how she'd walked over to Revco and bought a facial pack, a hot oil treatment, shaving cream, special lotion. She'd tried on all the sunglasses on the display rack but none were glamorous enough. And did Ginger know about the place in the mall where they gave you a makeover, changed you into a winter queen or a butterfly princess, and then took your picture like a model?

She gripped Ginger's hand and pulled her toward the bathroom, telling how she'd called the boy she liked, the one who was teaching his dog hand signals.

"At first he was shy, acted like he wanted to get off the phone," the girl said, "but then we started talking about dogs, how we both like big dogs and hate little yappy dogs, like poodles and Chihuahuas. I told him I wanted to live on a farm and have a lot of Labradors and golden retrievers." The girl spoke fast, as if talking was as fundamental to her survival as breathing. Ginger heard these endless monologues from older women at the church who lived alone—they were so afraid of self-reflection that they chatted endlessly—but never from such a young girl.

"How's your mother?" Ginger asked.

"Oh, she's a mess, turns out the dentist got *involved* with somebody while at a conference down in Florida. She came by with groceries, left me twenty dollars for lunch money, and said she'd be at his condo until further notice. They have to *talk things out* and they need, according to my mother, *to hold each other* at night." The girl stuck her finger down her throat in a gagging motion and shook her head. "Why anyone would want to kiss that bald-headed monster is beyond me. The guy reeks of fluoride and whenever I see him I hear the whir of the drill and see blood spinning around in that little porcelain sink."

She pulled Ginger through the doorway into the bathroom, where a beauty altar was set up on a peach towel next to the tub. Spread out evenly on the terry cloth, like instruments for an operation, were the spent tube of hair conditioner, a jar of purifying mud, a pink plastic disposable razor, and a small travel-size can of shaving cream. "I'm going to shave my legs."

"Don't do it," Ginger advised. "You'll be a slave to that razor forever."

"I don't care," the girl said, looking away, giving her neck a defiant twist. "My mother got me some cotton bra-and-panty sets."

"What does that have to do with anything?"

"And I already have my period," she said, kneeling next to the towel, as if that cemented the inevitability of this ritual. The girl looked over the beauty lotions as if they were wine and wafer.

"Do you want a beauty treatment too? I know a recipe for hair conditioner. You use half a can of beer and two raw eggs."

Ginger shook her head.

"Then you'll be the beautician?"

It was hard not to get caught up in the girl's goofy web of excitement. And besides, Ginger remembered when she was this age, how she'd heard that in the sixties women burned their bras. She was shocked and appalled. Bras, lipsticks, rouge, compacts, lacy nightgowns, and high-heel shoes, these were objects to wish for and revere. Ginger knelt down beside the towel.

The girl took off her quilted robe and sat up on the edge of the tub, spread her bare legs out in front of Ginger. She wore a tank top smattered with tiny red hearts and matching underwear. When she arched back, ribs striped her chest.

"Do it like the magazine says," the girl said, pointing at the lotion, "first a layer of this and then the shaving cream."

Ginger pumped the rose-scented lotion into her hand and spread it thickly over the girl's warm leg.

"Now the foam," she said, pointing at the can. "Don't you just love that stuff?" the girl said as foam piled up in Ginger's palm and she spread it over the cream, making sure every bit of skin was thoroughly covered. The pink razor pulled easily over the girl's skin. Ginger turned the tub water on and rinsed the blade. Greasy foam mixed with tiny blonde hairs splayed around the silver drain that reflected back a pockmarked picture of Ginger's face.

"Have you ever worn false eyelashes?" the girl asked as Ginger pulled the blade up again, careful around the nuance of ankle bone. "I'm a summer, don't you think?" her fingers stretched the skin over her cheek bones, "a summer with an oval face."

Ginger rinsed the blade again, glanced at the back of the girl's neck where a stork's bite splattered pink and the chain of her birthstone necklace lay delicately on her neck bone. She flexed her toes so Ginger could slide the razor around the tendon at the back of her foot. The dense foam, the rose-petal lotion, the double blades, and the cool pink skin put them both into a trance. Ginger threw her body forward as if experiencing a tiny electrical shock. The girl gave a puppy yelp and said accusingly, "You nicked me!"

"Shush," Ginger said, "I heard something." And there it was again, a passionate thump on the sliding glass doors downstairs.

"I told you this place was haunted," the girl said flatly as she examined the cut on the back of her foot, then pressed toilet paper over the wound.

It was alarming how much time lapsed between the thuds, enough time to run down a vagrant memory, to take a quick shower, or pour yourself a drink. Then the muffled thump happened again and the girl lifted her foot, blood gently soaking through the blue tissue paper.

"You better go down there and check it out." She said this so casually that Ginger thought for a moment that the girl had gotten a friend to pound intermittently on the window. She'd seen movies where the hero's mother, father, even sisters and brothers were all secret Satan worshipers, or cyborgs, or unfeeling aliens hatched out of space pods.

Up the hall and down the stairs, she started. The beige carpet had gray spots as if paper plates tipped and greasy hamburgers had flopped onto the synthetic shag. The mammalian scent of middle-class families floated in the hallway—over boiled broccoli, fabric softener, and the accumulated sweat of sleeping children. She stood in the middle of the rec room, a dark subterranean landscape populated with a Lazy Boy, vinyl dry bar, and the smelly couch where family members laid around like dogs in a cardboard box.

She waited, eyeing the framed poster of Monet's lily pads, the insipid colors and pretty flowers no different than Hallmark Easter cards. Nothing was down here, though as she turned, she saw a spot of red, a candy wrapper caught on a branch. Animated by the wind, it rose and sped directly toward her face. Like a shooting star with a mind of its own, like a lie come back to torment. Then the familiar thump and Ginger saw the cardinal, crazy eyed, hair stuck up on its head in tufts like a punk rocker.

The girl came down the stairs limping. Using scotch tape, she adhered a wad of Kleenex to her ankle. A thread of blood trickled over the pink arch of her foot.

"What was it?" She flopped her thin, ever-lengthening limbs onto the smelly couch.

"A bird," Ginger said.

The girl raised her eyebrows, her features rearranged to look incredulous. "Really?"

"Yeah." Ginger watched the girl lose interest.

"Let's pluck our eyebrows." She leaned forward. "I've read how if you use an ice cube to numb them it doesn't even hurt."

Her father's car was parked in Sandy Patrick's driveway, the light green Chrysler with the tiny Bibles in back, the box of Sunday school supplies, pipe cleaners and construction paper, Elmer's glue and Popsicle sticks. His clergy emergency sign was tucked up under the visor. He used it whenever he parked illegally. Thick gray cloud cover made the sky feel too close and there was a pathetic splattering of rain, drops so cold they reminded Ginger of the tin notes of a music box.

She crouched below the bay window, stood in the wood

chips beside a boxwood bush, and spied inside. Her father sat with Mrs. Patrick on the couch. Spread over the coffee table was a jelly glass glazed with Coke mist, an empty yogurt cup, and a Styrofoam take-out tray. Her father looked calm as he arranged the communion implements, and Ginger realized for weeks he'd probably stopped here on Mondays as part of his sick calls and hospital visits. Nearest Ginger's eye on the floor, a box overflowed with baby things, corduroy jumpers and little sweaters, a zip-lock bag of yellow hair and tiny baby teeth.

Wearing the traveling stole around his neck, her father raised the wafer, stamped with a dove, and Sandy's mother's head flopped forward in complete capitulation. He moved the wafer to her lips and her tongue darted out and took the wafer. Ginger's father tipped the tiny communion goblet to Sandy's mother's mouth, her throat shifting as she swallowed the wine. Her father's lips moved again, as he raised his hand up to his forehead, down past his chin, from shoulders, right to left, in the sad sign of the cross.

Sixteen: SANDY

"Stand still, if you want to look gorgeous," the butterfly said, as he applied mascara to the unicorn's long lashes, glittery purple eye shadow to his lids and pink nail polish to his marbled hoofs. The troll's mouth moved but no sound came out. He sat on the cellar steps and ate from a paper plate of hash browns drenched in ketchup.

"There's some for you," he said with his mouth full. "Don't you want it?" She smelled the onions, saw the lumps of potatoes he dumped onto the paper. She reached her hand out and brought the warm mush to her mouth. The food went down her sore throat like gravel. Pain laid on the newspapers like cold black stones. She was there only to contain and connect these sensations. When she looked over at the stairs, the troll was gone and the ridges of the brown cardboard gave off a little light. Had he been there at all? Or was that yesterday? She heard lead snakes racing over the wooden floor above her head and realized the troll was moving the furniture, pushing all the chairs and tables to the front of the house. The floorboards strained with the added weight and she imagined the house staggering forward, then sinking deeper into the mud.

When the unicorn came on stage he wore white bell-bottoms, his silk shirt unbuttoned to the navel, a gold chain dangling around his neck; the strobe lights went crazy as he sang a wild song about loneliness and love. In the closet, Sandy decided to let the boy put his hand up under her shirt. Dresses dangled above their heads as the boy slid his fingers over the skin of her stomach. Because he smelled like a zillion school lunches, she was afraid to touch him, instead bracing herself, one hand around the toe of a high heel, the other gripping the sole of a tennis shoe. The closet door swung open and the light let her see the expanse of newspapers spread over the basement floor and the pruning shears hung on a nail against the far wall.

"Keep it down," the troll said, then shut the door again. She pulled her knees closer to her chest and coughed so hard she choked up some bitter-smelling gunk. The troll opened the door again and rushed down the stairs, stood in the wedge of light, and glared at her. His eyes magnified by his glasses, his white beard made him look like the God of hash browns and cold pancakes.

The boy said he liked the drawing on her notebook of the unicorn and the butterfly with big doe eyes. She heard the TV going and opened her eyes to see the troll in a different shirt bending over in the far recesses of the basement. But by the time she opened her mouth, he disappeared. She heard him upstairs moving the furniture again; stone snakes raced across the ceiling. And something was in her mouth, mealy and sweet. It took a minute to recognize the flavor, narrow it down to a fruit, then land on the letters, arrange them, APPLE. The seeds and the stem were like bark against her teeth. But she swallowed these bits and let pee drizzle against her thigh, run down the crack of her rear. And then the poke of a bone against her cheek and she winced. The troll offered her a pork-chop bone with a bit of meat on the end. She grabbed it quick and ran across the floor, squatted in the corner and gnawed the fat. He sat on the stairs laughing, calling her his little monkey. Cute little monkey girl.

As the van paused at a red light, she glanced through the black curtains. Angels were strapped to every light post. Angels made of white shredded plastic, gold halos hovered above their flesh-tone heads. Their gowns were covered with car exhaust. Sandy recognized them from the highway in front of the mall. The van turned. Its tires wobbled like wagon wheels along an unpaved road. She was thrown up against something warm, something soft. The cat, she thought, and flipped her head to see the last bit of streetlight shine on a mess of shiny brown hair. It was Sandy Patrick dressed in footed pajamas with teddy bears on them. She was the little monkey, skinny as a pencil and covered with black and blues, and here was Sandy, ruddy-cheeked and almost chubby, her eyelids showing the spastic flicks that signaled REM sleep.

The van stopped and the troll turned off the engine. All she could hear was his breath coming from deep down in his murky lungs, and then he hacked some mucus out the window. Cars rushed down the highway and she heard the soft sound of snow gathering on the windshield.

The girl gave off a dry and comforting warmth like an electric blanket turned to the lowest setting. Wind hissed through the motorboat tarps, got caught in the ice-covered boards of the dock. Deep inside the green ice, a half-dead fish moved like a muscle spasm in the slushy body of water and the unicorn slipped as he landed on the man-made lake.

"Who will be with me?" she asked, but he pretended not to hear her, saying he'd just come by to give a quick hello, that he must hurry off as he was keynote speaker at the self-empowerment conference and already he'd missed the free baked chicken.

When he was as tiny as a bit of paper blown up into the sky, she watched the moon rise over the water. The skeleton baby waited inside. That bone baby would stay inside the moon forever. Only the dandelions kept changing from suns to moons, then back again.

Her nightgown broke up like tissue paper in water as he carried her back through the woods toward the cabin where the exhausted girls lay sprawled on their bunks. On the ground, books nobody wanted were encased in ice and she saw her blue feet, the nails like bits of hard candy. She felt a slight repulsion for them, like a plate of half-eaten food.

The cats, their fur the palest pink, each wore a necklace made of periwinkles and smoked cigarettes held in long rhinestone-studded holders. They sang in high trembling voices a sort of non-sense French and her little brother drew a unicorn with blue eye shadow and long silver lashes and he handed the picture to her and she thanked him and said she'd tape it up over her bed. It was easy really, these ideas, her mind, smoke-encased in ice. He threw the afghan onto the forest floor, spread the edges out with his foot, and laid her down near a pile of broken bricks.

"Shut up!" Sandy said, and the sound of her own voice, high-pitched and incoherent, terrified her.

"You must control your cough," the troll said, his hair a mass of ice-covered strands. But she hadn't realized she was coughing. He squatted down and put his hand to her throat, fingers feeling for the glands just at her jawline, under her ear. "Swollen up like lima beans," he smiled. "Poor little monkey." But then the smile flew off his face and his features went blank as a hollow-eyed statue and she felt all the air leaving her life like an inner tube with a pinprick leak. The ice broke under her weight and she sank down into the lake's cold water. Her hand clawed out, frenzied and separate, until she grasped the lava rock and sat up in her bed, poured white sugar in her palm so the deer would tongue her lifeline, her blue-veined wrist. It felt nice, his urgent animal tongue. But still she couldn't help thinking, *Is this all there is to it?*

The bear shook his head, took his hat off, looked down at her lying on the afghan spread over blue moss surrounded by broken plates. "My dear little girl," he said sadly, "what else did you expect?"

Seventeen: GINGER

A hand-painted cross, given to him by a Latin American missionary, hung above the spy hole of the door to her father's room at the welfare hotel. She heard his old black shoes moving around the room, murmuring on the thin carpet. Oystery pigeon poops covered the window ledge to her left. Across the street, on the steps of the old stone church, a bearded man slept below the arch of headless angels. So much happened so fast that Ginger felt disoriented.

The congregation voted for expansion and to add another pastor. Mulhoffer, her father said, delivered this information as if the decision was as important to the church's history as the signing of the Declaration of Independence was to America's. He'd actually made the last grandiose comparison and her father giggled nervously in a way that sounded, even to his own ears, a little bit satanic. A severance was arranged and he volunteered to vacate the parsonage immediately as long as his daughter could stay in the basement until the end of the month.

A door opened down the hall and a man, the one she'd seen weeks earlier in the hotel window, poked his head out. If people drank steadily and long enough they mutated into another species: frogish bleary eyes, noses like raw hamburger, a swimmy countenance brimming with longing and dread. He examined her jeans, her oversized jacket, her stringy hairdo and, deciding she was not altogether untrustworthy, smiled shyly.

"We already know all about Jesus," he said in a friendly, cheerful voice, cynicism edging only the last word. "You tell him that."

"Okay," Ginger said as the man turned back to his room and raised the volume on his TV set.

Her father opened the door wearing a white T-shirt pulled out over a pair of black preacher pants, his arms thin and white as a child's.

"Are the old guys harassing you?" he asked in a forced tone meant to dispel their mutual embarrassment.

Ginger shook her head. "The man with the brush cut wants me to tell you he knows all about Jesus."

Her father laughed, "He sure does. That guy's son died in Vietnam and his wife gave the family savings to a bounty hunter who said he'd bring the boy back alive." Ginger remembered him telling the story to her mother over dinner one night. Her father knew something secret about almost everyone in town. To hear these narratives was mesmerizing, but she worried that their accumulation had pushed her father over the edge.

He shook his head. "I gave the poor guy ten dollars, which your mother ridiculed me about for months."

Her mother loved to tell stories of how her father had been tricked; the guy who said he had sleeping sickness, the man selling electric flashlights, the woman who came to the church office saying she needed money because her baby was sick.

He moved a pile of books so she could sit on the bed. Ginger forgot that the furniture in the house all belonged to the church and she was shocked by how little he had, a few boxes of theology books—one marked sermons contained thousands of legal pad pages. The folded blanket from the church office sat neatly at the end of the bed. On the card table by the window he set up an altar. Both his paintings, the ark in the gloomy canal and the dark forest topped by celebratory lilies, leaned up against the glass. Before them he arranged his round-faced bust of Martin Luther, the bronze praying hands, his Oxford Bible, and a set of silver candleholders he'd given her mother one year for Christmas. Leaning against the tarnished metal was a curling snapshot of Sandy Patrick in her brownie uniform, a big goofy smile spread over her face.

Ginger knew he and Ruth Patrick had become good friends. He used her minivan to move and last week Ginger saw them eating together at a fast-food place along the highway. She knew the tinfoil-covered paper plates of star-shaped sugar cookies and lemon squares came from Mrs. Patrick's kitchen. Even now, an open Tupperware container of brownies sat on top of the muted TV.

"What's going on at the house?" her father asked as if the

energy of his delivery could distract her from the half-eaten food and the room's general dinginess.

"They steamed off the wallpaper in the dining room yesterday and today they're tearing up all the carpet."

Her father's pupils dilated and he got that spacey, nostalgic look. The ranch house had always been an embarrassment to him, the fake-wood paneling and hokey intercom system. Her mother had wanted to fix it up, but there was never any money to do it right, have drapes made, buy a proper couch. So the living room stood empty, just a ficus plant in one corner beside her father's pile of old *New York Times*.

"What about my room? Your mother had that shade of blue mixed especially."

"The minister's wife is going to paint the whole house beige. She wants to give the place a country look."

Her father looked confused.

"Dollies, quilts, silk flower arrangements in antique flour mills." Ginger remembered the petite woman with the teddy bear on her cotton sweater, her features set in a stagy display of empathy as she asked questions about the water stain under the kitchen sink.

"Oh dear," her father grimaced. "God does work in mysterious ways."

Ginger laughed sharp and flat as a gunshot. She was so relieved he could still joke that her shoulders slipped down and she let a long breath up from her lungs.

"Best to get out of there as soon as you can," he continued. She hadn't told her father yet, but she'd been thinking of moving in with Ted. Since he disappeared, she thought of him like a delicate and slightly demented prince. She missed their late-night talks about

time travel and getting his navel pierced. Distance gave him a nar-
cotic and slightly saintly appeal.

"So have you decided what *you're* going to do?" Ginger asked.
The night of the news, his emphatic, wild-eyed ideas frightened her.
He was going to Haiti to work with the poor; he was going to min-
ister to the homeless and live among them on the streets.

His neck flushed a prickly nervous pink, and his face grew
even paler. "Well, you know the economy is not what it used to be,"
he glanced at the picture of a beach put into a dime-store frame and
hung over the sagging twin bed, "and I'm not a young man either."

Ginger nodded as he brought the Oxford Bible onto his lap
and pulled out a glossy pamphlet. "I'm thinking of something along
these lines, where my experience would come in handy." He passed
her the rectangle of slick-colored paper.

PEACE OF MIND, the pamphlet spelled out in soft blue pastel
letters, the typeface cursive and feminine. Inside was a photograph
of a synthetic stone gate with two azalea bushes on either side of a
newly paved asphalt drive. Above hung an iron sign with gold letters: Forest Rest Cemetery. Opposite the photo was a checklist,
reasons why a cemetery plot was a good investment.

"I don't get it. You're going to work at the cemetery?"

Her father leaned back on the folding chair, one she knew
he'd taken from the church basement. "No. No. I'll be selling plots
door to door."

He was tired. He was not himself. "You're kidding, right?"
Ginger asked.

"Not at all." A smile bit into his cheeks, its rigid architec-
ture all that held him up. Instead of moving into one of the condos
on the highway, he moved to this monkish room in a sleazy hotel and

decided to do the job that most made his skin crawl. Grief sent her father into this alternate reality.

Ginger handed the pamphlet back. "You have gone completely nuts," she said, spacing out each word for effect.

"Maybe so." He looked down at the photo as if considering the possibility. Yellow stains were burned under the arms of his T-shirt and his eyes looked wet and confused, their expression not unlike those of the hotel's other shell-shocked residents.

"You know," he said, "it's true what your mother used to say. I have no idea how the world works."

Even from the grave her mother's endless accusations, long rooted in her father's head, grew up like goat grass through cracks in cement. Her father always countered her mother by saying she was chained like a slave to the world of things. But Ginger knew all she wanted was to be respectable, have a clean couch in her living room and a few nice dresses hanging in her closet.

"If you could have heard Mulhoffer," her father's own voice trembled.

"Who cares?" Ginger asked. "The man is a moron."

Admiration filtered across his face but then the light drained out of his eyes. He'd decided there was no use trying to explain. "Of course you're right," he said unconvincingly, his head swiveling like an adolescent's over her shoulder to the muted TV.

He bolted up and raised the volume. "Did you hear?" he asked, his eyes locked to the screen. "Another girl is missing."

Ginger swung around on the bed, watched the video footage of police in black rain slickers being led by German shepherds on leashes through the woods.

"Who is it?"

"Shush," her father nodded at the newscaster, a young man who jumbled his vowels and looked a little too excited as he delivered the facts. Police were searching the woods between Willow Brook subdivision and Creek Mist Condo Complex, where neighbors said kids sometimes played. The screen flashed to the house, a mint-green split-level. Press gathered under black umbrellas on the front lawn. The mother provided home-video footage; flickering and fuzzy sun dappled a picnic table covered with a red gingham cloth. And then the girl, a towheaded child with slate blue eyes in a strappy sundress, turned toward the camera. "Oh my God," Ginger said, "I know that girl."

Press vans lined the street in front of the girl's house, their white satellite dishes collecting cold drizzle. Inside one of the campers, a pinched-faced woman sat typing intently into her laptop computer. And inside a bland rental car, an older man talked on his cellular phone, glancing occasionally at his legal pad notes. The rain kept most of the media inside their vehicles, though she overheard two men in parkas standing outside a minivan talking about Sandy Patrick.

Smoke leaked from the carport next door to the girl's house, where a teenaged boy grilled hot dogs and filled his entrepreneurial cooler with Diet Cokes, and on the front lawn neighbors stood in little groups under umbrellas. Ginger saw two girls holding a candle and looking solemnly up at the house. A young female newscaster stood under a striped CBS umbrella and complained to the cameraman that Oprah had already offered the mother big money for an exclusive and she heard Maury Povich had checked into the Hilton out by the airport.

A truck from the local TV station was parked in the drive-way. Thick black cords ran out the back end, over the cement walk and through the front door. Ginger leaned inside, saw two men sitting below six screens, simultaneously showing a woman with the same fine features as her daughter say, ". . . please, whoever you are, let my little girl go. She's all I have in this world and I——." Her mouth trembled, refused to make words, formed into the primordial O, and she stuck a Kleenex to her lips and pressed her head into the neck of the bald dentist. His little pony tail shifted, the one the girl always referred to as a rat's tongue.

The man inside the truck swiveled his chair around to face the other man sitting in front of the soundboard. "Bet you ten to one," he said, "that little girl is already dead."

"T-R-O-U-B-L-E!" the hippie spelled out, leaning out the screen door of his white house. The smell of rich dirt and sweet pot blossoms wafted around him. "That's what we called the spooky little girls down on the commune. There was one I remember who wore nothing but men's shirts, always had field flowers hanging out of her hair, and told everybody she was Jesus' little sister." The hippie shook his head. "Man, it's like I'm trying to tell you, everything is out of whack."

"I need to keep looking," Ginger said. She didn't have time to hear one of the hippie's apocalyptic manifestos. "Maybe she's waiting back at my house."

The hippie looked skeptical. "Just don't call the police," he said. "She'll turn up next week at the bus station in Palo Alto and the next thing you know we'll see her on *Entertainment Tonight* hanging on the arm of some movie star."

"You think?" Ginger said hopefully.

"Sure," the hippie said, "that's what always happened to all those girls, either that," his loopy smile tensed, "or something else."

No, he hadn't seen the girl, though she'd taken to calling him late in the night, singing her favorite songs to him over the telephone and asking if she could come over to score, Steve said as they stood in the living room, just inside the door. He wore a towel around his waist, seemed bored, kept his eyes half closed, his mouth slack.

"She's a freaky chick," he said. "For all I know she could have walked into the woods and killed herself."

"Did she say she was going to do that?"

"She said a lot of crazy stuff. How do I know?" he said, glancing down the hall, where Ginger suspected a woman waited in his bed, one of the older ladies who bought him tanks of gasoline and took him out for steak.

Her room was empty. Her sleeping bag wadded up on the bottom sheet, a fine layer of plaster dust covering everything from where the workmen were putting up drywall in the corner. Ginger flopped down on her bed. She held on to this picture, to the exclu-

sion of any thought or sensation, the girl sprawled on her bed sleeping deeply like a child, sweat dampening the nape of her neck. But
now this last hope dissolved, leaving her sick with worry. Clenching her eyes shut so hard the usual silver blackness turned to orange,
she heard blood thumping in her ears. *Please God bring her back* and
she saw the girl walking around the mall with ten dollars in her pocket
for an orange julius and a pair of earrings, the girl scratching a bug
bite on the back of her calf and laughing in that self-conscious way
she thought of as glamorous, talking about super- models, her favorite Cindy, getting her hair soft as silk pajamas, and the aggres-
sive way she yanked perfume samples out of magazines. *If you bring
her back,* she prayed to God, *I'll take care of her myself.* She imagined
him like a black hole with a swirly ghost face and a booming, com-
puterized voice. Better to pray to Jesus and his bullet-riddled body,
blood trickling from the corner of his mouth.

Highway lights illuminated falling ice like patches of free-
form static, and the crimson Steak and Ale sign floated up on the
hill like a message from an angry God. Rain turned to ice, so the
asphalt was slick as oil, and the few cars on the road slid like old dogs
trying to keep their balance. Ginger's umbrella blew back with a tug.
Several ribs were broken so she pitched it down into the muddy ditch.
Slushy water moved sluggishly into a drainage pipe. Drops of ice hit
her face in a sensation cold and sharp but not altogether unpleasant.
Mud froze up in ridges like whipped cream, made soft crushing sounds under the heels of her tennis shoes. Branches rattled
against one another like dime-store wind chimes as she moved onto

the dirt path past the cat skeleton and the broken-down high chair. Ice glazed the old socks and bits of newspaper, froze bugs to dead leaves, and gathered in mealy drifts on the ground.

The barn was dark. She'd half hoped Ted would be in front of the fire, reading the I-Ching and toasting marshmallows. Ashes surrounded the TV like a moat; plastic carnations scattered over the dirt floor. Moving the toe of her tennis shoe around in the ash, she felt for the deer's head, but it was gone. A sheet of newspaper fluttered at the edge of the ash, diaphanous and nuanced as a scarf, a phantom with a white face. Startled, she thought someone said something, but when she turned her head all she heard was the rain's flat report on the soggy papers in the corner. Drips formed a discordant melody and entered her mind like speech. She listened to the wind flap against the dead leaves on the forest floor. She felt stupid now for thinking the girl might be here. The hippie was probably right: she was headed for Colorado or California or any one of those states that looked pretty in photographs. Wearing headphones, reading a magazine, the girl was probably curled into a seat on a dark and buoyant nighttime bus.

Wind spun the branches against one another like a chaotic chandelier. Ginger walked out the barn doorway, stood looking into the woods, thought another deer might be moving among the trees, or the ghost deer had come back to haunt the woods, searching for its head. Coming around the side of the barn, she saw a figure and though at first she couldn't make out the features, she presumed it was Ted, but then stray condominium light showed a small hunched man with a long white beard and bulging eyes. Anger shot off him, dense and oppressive as an opened oven door, as he yanked her arm so hard the bone wheezed and strained against her shoulder socket.

He swung his arm up and hit her in the face, thumb jabbing into her eye, the ridge of his fingers breaking the bridge of her nose. Blood ran into her mouth and she felt dizzy.

"What?" She didn't understand.

"Shut the fuck up!" He dragged her around the back side of the barn where his van was parked, the back doors open. Rain fell onto her hot face. Squares of condo-complex light floated like luminous fish back in the woods. She screamed until her whole head vibrated, blood flooding the valley beneath her tongue, and she slid deep into herself, searched room to room: the flashlight's beam illuminated a scattered pile of jigsaw-puzzle pieces and a pot filled with old rice. The tip of a branch caught her arm, bowed then snapped, sent shards of ice flying. The man threw her inside the van, where the girl lay bound and stretched on a mattress, her pupils shiny and huge as moons reflected in water. Ginger rolled her butt up, flexed her feet, and kicked hard at the troll's chest. He sucked air, staggered sideways. The girl screamed through her gag, vowels and consonants mumbled and undecipherable as animal speech. Ginger tried to pull her up at the waist, but the girl's wrists and ankles were secured with a piece of cord that ran underneath the mattress. She yanked at the cord, as the girl thrashed her head back and forth, tears leaking out the corners of her eyes. There was no give and Ginger heard the troll rattling the foliage just behind her, his breath rasping up from his lungs. She turned, saw the raised knife gleam then felt a tug at the side of her mouth and a soft sound like lettuce ripping, and above her head the sky filled with radiant light, illuminating the veiny backs of leaves, and she thought, *It's an angel coming down to save me.* Branches quivered and shook as four white horse legs broke through the green canopy and the unicorn flapped its luscious white wings in a succession of tiny flutters that allowed him to land expertly on the van's roof. A brown bear wearing a bow tie, its paws entwined in the long mane hair, rode bareback.

"This really is the best way to travel," the bear said to the glittery blue butterfly with the long eyelashes pausing on the shoulder of his dinner jacket.

"I couldn't agree with you more," the little fellow replied in a tiny voice, distinct as a cricket's.

The two went on about the plebeian inelegance of plane travel, the gray waiting areas, the pathetic airport bars. "Every place is the same place," said the bear, "so it's idiotic really to fly around everywhere." And then like a radio nudged off its channel to chaotic static, to the exclamations of right-wing preachers and basement revolutionaries, Ginger couldn't make out what anyone was saying anymore. She commanded her eyes to open and after a long while, at their leisure, her lids crept up. The van was gone and she felt so light-headed she thought she'd throw up as she pushed herself off the forest floor and staggered out of the tree line to the first lit window. Inside, an older woman sat at her kitchen table, reading a handwritten letter surrounded by snapshots of a baby. The portable TV on the table was tuned to QVC. Fear blossomed on the woman's face and Ginger saw her own monstrous reflection, blood streaming out of her nostrils, her cheek a raised puddle of raw purple flesh.

"Help me!" she screamed and the woman's eyes lost their wide-eyed worry, grinded down into maternal concern as she rushed around the corner toward the sliding glass door. "Oh my God," she said, "just a minute."

EPILOGUE

While she waited for the memorial service to begin, a little blonde girl, encouraged by her mother, placed a teddy bear beside a wreath of pink roses. If Ginger hadn't turned down the familiar road between the two strip malls, she wouldn't have recognized the dump. The new parking lot was filled with Saturns and minivans and the white gravel path that led past a cement birdbath and a wooden bench to the park's center, to these stones arranged like a child's game of hopscotch and covered now with tokens of bereavement: stuffed bunnies and baby dolls, carnations wrapped in cellophane, candles burning in tall glass holders, Hallmark sympathy cards and homemade construction paper ones sitting upright on the slabs of stone.

Her father and Ruth Patrick shook hands with the reporter from the local television station and made their way around the home-made shrine. He wore his black preacher pants, a white clerical collar, and over these a blue and white seersucker jacket, a gift, Ginger figured, from Ruth Patrick. His letters to Ginger in the hospital had detailed the construction of the Rose Hill Farm retirement complex behind the mall and the Pirates Cove Putt Putt next door to the mega-church, and how the chamber of commerce tore down the barn, hauled away all the garbage, and thinned the trees to create this memorial park. He rarely mentioned Ruth Patrick, but Ginger knew by his change of address that they had moved in together and that he'd given up the cemetery job and was going back to the community college for his teaching certificate.

"Let us bow our heads," he began, his church voice all the more resonant for lack of use. "Dear Father in Heaven, we pray that this gathering will honor your endless gifts of bountiful love. Amen." He lifted his eyes and scanned the faces in the crowd with his unnerving composure. "This spring has been bittersweet. While crocuses and daffodils rise and the buds of the maple press out into leaves," he motioned to the red and yellow tulips swaying in a bed at the park's far corner, "it's as if we've lost a part of ourselves as elemental as our hand or our foot, and this loss shakes us." He paused a moment. "So let us pray for the safe return of all missing children and for the lost souls who perpetrate these evil acts. Every human soul is a part of God and we must have mercy when we see that one of his holy sparks has been lost in a maze and is almost stifled." Her father unclasped his hands and looked above the crowd, his voice less serious, invested now with enthusiasm and hope. "Today we gather together to throw off the miserable blanket of despair and celebrate the memory of Sandy Patrick, a girl with a soul as expansive as this blue sky above."

Her father gave Ruth Patrick a questioning look and she nodded, took a step forward, unfolded an index card, and glanced down, then up again. "Thank you all for coming today," her voice shaky. "It means so much to me and my son. It means a lot that you're here to honor Sandy and that in your hearts she will live on forever. We miss her still, but knowing that so many people care has helped us both very much. I thank you." She paused and looked over at Ginger's father, who nodded encouragement. "As we were going through Sandy's things, we found several poems she had written, and my son Andrew would like to read one now."

The thin boy in the new blue suit and clip-on tie didn't raise his eyes to the crowd, just started to read fast, rushing the words together in a way that implied if he'd wanted to read the poem before, now, in front of the crowd, he felt embarrassed.

> *The bear said to the butterfly,*
> *"Come back and be my friend."*
> *The butterfly said, "No I won't,*
> *we've come now to the end."*

The poem went on about a brown bear and a place where butterflies sang and cattails were pink and ducklings yellow. She imagined Sandy's soul, like diaphanous cotton candy charged with static.

* * *

Switching off the lamp with the lace shade, Ginger pulled back the comforter, and got into bed. She was relieved the sheets weren't swarming with Little Mermaids. Downstairs, Ruth Patrick and her father sat quietly together on the couch in the basement, waiting for the spot about the memorial service on the eleven o'clock news, and she heard the boy snoring in the room next door. After the service he'd thrown a piece of gravel at a little girl, and when his mother yelled, he'd started crying and continued in the car all the way back to the house.

Ginger opened the jewelry box on the little table beside the bed. A tiny ballerina popped up, bits of lace for her skirt, a dab of pink paint for a bodice, a dab of brown for her bun, moving in circles on the tips of her toes to the tinkling notes of a lullaby. Ginger looked out the window at the houses spinning out in curly cul-de-sacs like the paisleys the orderly at the hospital called Tears of the Buddha. She remembered the shining police lights, the frenzied dogs, saliva stringing off their pink gums, and the tiny emaciated creature lying on the afghan, strands of her hair encased in ice. Eyes staring through the broken bricks and ice-covered ferns. Smeared with feces and covered with spider bites, Sandy's face strange and shrunken like a blue gray cat's, already transported to the nether world, a wood nymph or a forest fairy, found only inside the pages of a children's book.